James Monro hunts the ghost
of Jack the Ripper
London 1888

James Monro hunts the ghost of Jack the Ripper

"I'm not **a butcher**, I'm not a **Yid**,
Nor yet a **foreign Skipper**.
But I'm **your own light-hearted friend**,
Yours truly, Jack the Ripper"

Anonymous 1888

James Monro hunts the ghost of Jack the Ripper

James Monro hunts the ghost of Jack the Ripper

London 1888

Patrick Van gerdinge; author
Vince Palace; narrator
Anne Gaelle Mercier; english translation

James Monro hunts the ghost of Jack the Ripper

Main characters:

- James Monro; (1838-1929), main narrator, speaking in
the first person.
Education: Edinburgh High School, University of Berlin.
Wedding: Ruth Littlejohn 1863.
June 1882: Commissioner of the Bengal Presidency, return London
July 1884: Deputy Commissioner of Criminal Affairs of Scotland
Yard.

- Melville Macnaghten; (1853-1921), friend of James
Monro, met in India during their respective stay.
Arrived in London in the spring of 1888.

- Sir Charles Warren; chief commissioner of
Scotland Yard. Superior hierarchical James Monro;
with whom he has conflicting relations.

- Frederick Abberline; inspector Scotland Yard,
seconded to Whitechapel's H division,
to investigate the repeated murders of prostitutes.

James Monro hunts the ghost of Jack the Ripper

1

James Monro; Calcutta 1882

I was appointed by the Government of England as Judge, officiating at Jessore province of Bengal April 10 1877. In January 1878 I became Inspector General of the Bengal Police, then Divisional Commissioner of the Presidency on June 14 in 1882; I met Melville Leslie Macnaghten, who was 25 years old. He was the son of Elliot Macnaghten, who had allowed me to have this high office in India and I was happy to be able to protect his 15th son in this land of Bengal.

He had arrived in Bombay on a 21-day long voyage in October 1873 to his property in Kichnaghur; 110 km north of Calcutta. A few years later he returned to London at the request of his father Elliot to marry Dora Emily Sanderson, Reverend Robert Edward Sanderson's daughter, on October 3, 1878. As soon as they returned home to India, Dora had her first child, Charles Melville, on November 18, 1879. Shortly afterwards, the Macnaghten couple conceived a second child in December 1880.

During Dora's pregnancy in May 1881; an accident occurred that changed the life of Melville. When Lord Ripon's royal taxes were lifted, agitators manipulated the minds of the peasants. A printed document was sent to all the houses of the farmers of Lower Bengal, saying it was from the Lord Sahib stating that rents should be paid, and that if, after receiving this notice, a Muslim paid this tax he would be driven to hell, and in the case of a Hindu, that the two sons of Siva would eat his head.

Thus, this text froze the Hindu and Muslim blood. In many areas the rioters refused to pay and in some districts their attitude was so threatening that the Zemindars (owners) and Macnaghten left the Bengal plains for a few months and temporarily migrated to the healthiest and most peaceful hills from the north around Darjeeling. Back in Kishnaghur, Melville had been told that a man had chaired his village committee, violently threatening farm workers. Melville, still having a duty to do a local and personal survey, went directly to the village to talk to the farmers. A winemaker had crept up behind him and hit him with a club, so hard that Melville fell unconscious to the ground. He had been brought completely unconscious to his home by his men. (1)

(1) Days of my Years - Melville Macnaghten 1914

The blow had rattled Melville's brain, but he hadn't realized at the time that the blow to the head was going to lead to a complete change in his life. Later he was able to return to the village with the police, to identify the many ringleaders. Warned, Governor of Bengal Sir Ashley Eden had severely punished the rioters and the man who beat Melville.

After a few months, Dora gave birth to little Julia Mary on September 10, 1881. (2)

For my part, on June 14, 1882, I had been appointed sub-commissioner of the Bengal police. On this occasion I had met and forged a long friendship with Melville and his family. They lived in Kishnaghur, a few miles from my district of Nuddea.

After numerous requests to return to London, on July 7, 1884, I had finally been appointed to succeed Sir C.E. Howard Vincent as Deputy Commissioner of the Metropolitan Police in charge of the Department of Criminal Investigations.

On leaving India for London, I promised Melville Macnaghten that I would do my best to find him a post as Assistant Chief of Police at Scotland Yard.

(2) http://www.thepeerage.com/p2334.htm#i23331

Melville took advantage of this trip to bring his two children back to the land of their grandfather Elliot and to his beautiful home, "Ovingdean House". The two children would quickly start school in Brighton and then in London. (*)

(*) A Wiser Woman? Christabel Macnaghten 1966

2
James Monro; London 1888

Having been posted in London for 4 years, I took advantage of a hiring period at Scotland Yard, to propose for my friend Melville Macnaghten, an assistant position. On March 29, 1888, the Ministry confirmed the appointment of Macnaghten to this position so much desired by my friend.

James Monro

I was immediately informed, of the good news by a letter on March 30, 1888. A special porter for the Nuddea district brought this letter in April 1888 to Mr. Melville Macnaghten in the town of Kishnaghur.

 He immediately arranged to leave Bengal as soon as possible and return to London with his wife Dora and their servants. The two lovely children, eight-year-old Charles and six-year-old Julia, had already been sent to England to begin their studies.

In Bombay, on the eighteenth of April, at five o'clock in the morning, the Macnaghten family embarked on the Clyde, from the Peninsular & Oriental shipping company (P & O). This magnificent steamer, a hundred and nineteen meters long, had been built to pass through the Suez Canal. On the morning of the sixth day he made a stop in Aden's cove. Against a few rupees, the Macnaghten landed to visit the hydraulic works of the city. An hour later, the Clyde was setting anchor towards the Red Sea.

After another four days sailing in a sea strewn with shipwrecks, the Clyde eventually reached the Gulf of Suez. After ten days, the steamship took the narrow Suez Canal pierced by the French, at the initiative of Ferdinand Lesseps.

The ship was following the lights marking the two banks; she arrived at Port Said in the evening. In the early morning the ship returned to sea to reach the southern Italian port of Brindisi in three days, the final step of this long sea voyage. The family took place in the comfortable cars of the Peninsular express to finally arrive in London early May 1888.

In the meantime, my superior Sir Charles Warren, chief commissioner of Scotland Yard, inquired about Melville's past.

Charles Warren

He learned that in India Macnaghten was mistreating his men, and in 1881, by revenge, an Indian had stunned him with a blow, the supreme indignity for a subject of Her Majesty the Queen. (*)

(*) Days of my Years - Melville Macnaghten 1914 p 50

Sir Charles Warren, who had given a favourable opinion on Macnaghten's appointment in April, suddenly changed his mind after he became aware of these events; Sir Melville Macnaghten would not have the post; Charles Warren would oppose his appointment. Unable to warn Melville; I found myself in an embarrassing situation.

That Wednesday, May 2, at Scotland Yard, I waited for my friend's visit, without knowing how to announce this sad news.

Suddenly there was a knock on the door; three firms quick and determined blows.

Sir Melville Macnaghten

"Come in!"

The door opened slowly and Melville appeared in the frame. I got up from my chair and walked around the desk; my arms warmly extended to my friend.

"That good old Macnaghten!"

The returned traveller from Bengal leaned his shoulders squarely to me, and a benevolent smile rolled up the ends of his finely trimmed officer's moustache.

"James my friend."

"Always so dashing!"

Melville is thirty-five years old, tanned, broad-shouldered, a dry and energetic handshake. He is a man in the prime of life. I'm head of Scotland Yard's Criminal Investigations Department, and if I did not have the title officially, everyone considered me as the deputy commissioner. It was not without pretension that I drove him to my private office. The walls were covered with curiosities brought back from the Raj; horns of beasts oriental weapons, framed clippings, various trophies. My files were piled up on large shelves. My desk was very different from the empty austerity of the rest of the Yard. In the corridors the Bobbies and the officials swarmed loudly. On the wall of my office, my diplomas and decorations adorned the wooden panels. I was proud of my education at the University of Edinburgh.

It was only by cultivating every relationship, from school benches to maharaja ballrooms; that gradually; patiently; tirelessly; I was able to rise to this level of respectability judge and inspector general of the Bengal Police. There the Indians nicknamed me, the black Cobra Sahib.

Suddenly, Melville froze as he entered my office. I followed his gaze, which fixed a rack resting on a filing cabinet. He put his fists on his hips in a resolute contemplative position.

"Beautiful, isn't it?"

Melville just nodded silently.

"Double gutter" he said.

The rack supported a curved Nepalese dagger, used by our Ghurkha regiments. A functional, perfectly balanced weapon, witch I had forged by a Calcutta gunsmith, just before leaving the dampness of Bengal. At this moment, the unaltered blade sends back a slice of our faces, the austere cheekbones of my friend, my placid eyebrows, and my budding baldness.

"A kukri ..." he said.

He leaned forward to read the small plaque, just below, which recalled the object's origin. I watched this rapacious look; his icy eyes seemed to stare at the death of the beast collapsing under his blows.

He put his hands in the pockets of his elegant three-piece suit, turned around, with a carnivorous smile.

"There is no better knife to serve the pig!" He said, miming a kukri movement piercing an imaginary boar with a quick and precise gesture, a kukri movement piercing an imaginary boar!

"Useless when we run after leopards!" I said pleasantly.

"But practical to disembowel jackals and reward the good work of dogs by giving them the best offal" He says with conviction.

He giggled and put a hand on my shoulder. Then he sat down in front of my desk; looking at me quietly, vaguely happy; waiting for the conversation to begin.

"London in June should seem cold." I said!

"Oh yes. I'm not unhappy about wearing these clothes," he said, pulling on the lapels of his jacket.

A slight silence followed our futile exchanges and then Melville entered the heart of the matter.

"How is the activity of Scotland Yard in our beloved Metropolis?" He said with a detached air.

"Terrible, my dear, terrible! I have work beyond my possibilities. The city is an odious shambles. The scoundrel of the East End is stifling all the holy day, when she does not throw herself on honest people."

19

Lately we have had problems with soldiers who found nothing better than to stab a poor Whitechapel girl with a bayonet. Such savagery!   (*)

"I have a lot to do, my friend!" My men are competent but I am seriously lacking in numbers.

I looked defiantly through the wall of the wall towards Charles Warren's office.

"Not to mention that this ... ugly commissioner puts me in the wheel."

"I'm not particularly interested in the work of the inspectors!" These are the last words of Charles Warren! He cares very little about our men on the ground!

"I've never met the man face to face, but I already know he doesn't meet the expectations of royalty, does he?"

"He is hated, rigid and brutal. This past winter, Sunday, November 13, he clubbed the crowd in Trafalgar Square, one dead and several hundred wounded. In the press they called the event Bloody Sunday; a disgrace for the Crown."

If it had been possible, I would rather not have met him. What organization! It did not happen like that in the Calcutta Special Branch.

Melville said nothing and kept looking at me with the same ruthless predator look he had while observing the kukri.

(*)Martha Tabram August 7, 1888, killed 39 shots at George Yard Building.

20

He seemed to collect and weigh each of my words. The impression he stared at caught me at the moment of my diatribe against the Principal Commissioner, and this sensation finally made me come to the point:

"I made you come to help me! Charles Warren is out of place among us. I need a person under my command to counter his inept methods..."

You are someone who possesses discipline, rigor, and obstinacy. But I also need a bloodhound, doubled by a hunter!

"That's what you told me in your letter dated April 30, 1888, James! So is there a post for me?"

"Absolutely, my dear Melville, I ask you solemnly and officially to accept the post of chief of the police officers of the city of London. I have gathered all the necessary signatures including that of Minister Henry Matthews."

But only Warren is a problem.

"What problem?"

"Nothing really bad, I'll have to easily change my mind."

Melville stared at me with piercing eyes.

"Devil, I think that in memory of our relationship in Bengal, I can not refuse such an honorary position. It is with joy that I will help you!"

This last sentence was pronounced, with all the solidity of sincerity.

"Good, perfect," I say. I am satisfied that you accept this work.

"Seriously James I would not have made this journey from Kishnaghur, if I had not wanted this post of deputy commissioner of the capital of the empire! Great God!"

"Do not cry victory right away. It is still necessary for Warren to accept my new request. You have an appointment with him very soon; early June. I would come with you!"

"Well James, let's talk about more cheerful things. What festivities are currently taking place in this old London?"

"Ha... rascal. You are an incorrigible rascal. Just arrived and you already want to beat the pavement like a young dandy single. We did not even mention Dora and your two children!"

"Oh! They are doing well: like angels! So, what's interesting?" He enthused.

"Alas, we will never save the soul of poor Melville Macnaghten! Well, old man, there are many possible outings. Do you still like the theatre?"

"I plead guilty!"

"In this case why not this?"

I raised a few sheets on my desk and pulled out a program that I slid under the eyes.

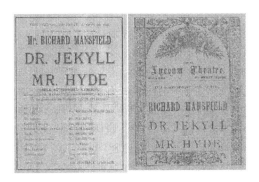

"It's a friend who gave me this. It seems that the interpretation will be surprising. The premiere will take place on Saturday, August 4. We should go, what do you think?"

Melville's eyes fixed on the paper, to open wide. Dr. Jekyll and Mr. Hyde are given at the Lyceum theatre with Richard Mansfield as Principal. (*)

"Richard Mansfield!" His face lit up like a child surprised by a splendid present.

"Richard Mansfield, I confirm!"

Melville took the program with both hands. He studied it conscientiously but this time with an air of simple joy which I had never seen in him.

(*)*L'étrange cas du docteur Jekyll et de M. Hyde de Robert Louis Stevenson*

23

I glanced at my pocket watch which indicated to me at the end of the morning, our interview was coming to an end.

"It's a great idea!" He said, straightening up, not taking his eyes off the sheet.

"In this case it is decided; I will immediately reserve the places."

I patted his back cordially, while bringing him back to the exit.

"Do you know, James, that I've always been passionate about drama?"

"I suspected it!"

"I even took to the stage in my younger days!"

On the doorstep, he continued to rehearse his memories. Shakespeare, Ben Johnson, Mansfield. I was going to grab his hand to say goodbye, when he exclaimed:

"I would remember all my life when I announced to my "father" that I wanted to pursue a career as an actor."

"What did he answer?"

"Nothing! Then he looked at me over his glasses, his glassy eyes, for an infinite time…"

"That's all?"

"He ended up saying: "It seems to me that you are perfectly crazy; you can do what you want"

Melville imitates the calm and solemn tone of Sir Elliott Macnaghten, the head of the East India Company, so well that I burst out laughing. I shook my friend's hand warmly, and he stepped out.

By nightfall Scotland Yard was still teeming with police officers, wizards and victims, mingling in a mixture of tweed, cotton, quality wood, shapeless garments and starched uniforms.

I went back to my office to continue my mail exchanges with Charles Warren in order to make him bend; Melville had to get this job as I had promised him.

I wrote him the following letter:

On May 4th, James Monro (MEPO 4/487): (*)

"I regret that I can not approve your statements that I have no official knowledge of Mr. Macnaghten's appointment.

To the extent that this information reaches me, I can not admit that you can give me a warning about my conduct. I am not mistaken as to the nature of the relationships I must have with you, as Commissioner, and I do not understand what gave you reason to believe otherwise. You are mistaken when you say that while I was in the department, I heard Mr. Ruggles Brise say that the Secretary of State had approved the appointment of Mr. Macnagthen.

(*) « The National Archives » de Kew : MEPO 4/487

This information was given to me by Mr. Ruggles Brise himself, in my office at 21 Whitehall Place. I communicated this decision to Mr. Macnagthen in the forms, and with the assurance that you had likewise, your recommendation to this gentleman. I was not aware of your withdrawal regarding the offer of this post to Mr. Macnaghten. I still believe that this withdrawal was later than the decision of the Secretary of State, in that your decision was communicated to me only weeks after the commission, in your memo of April 23 or 24.

Having been officially notified of the post, it seems to me that I acted in a justified manner. I do not see how I made a mistake, and by the same token, it seems impossible to do anything for me to blame myself»

On May 7, from Sir Charles Warren to James Monro (HO 144/190 / A46472B): (*)

"I would appreciate it if in the future you were courteous enough to keep copies of your correspondence with the Ministry, and if you could, as Assistant Commissioner, keep track of your verbal exchanges, to keep me informed. The days of what is happening »

(*) The National Archives » de Kew: (HO 144/190 / A46472B)

On May 9, James Monro responds (HO 144/190 / A46472B): (*)

"I regret not being able to follow up on your request. It seems to me that such a request is based on an error of interpretation concerning the duties inherent to my function as assistant commissioner in charge of intelligence»

On May 9, from Sir Charles Warren to Henry Matthews, Minister (HO 144/190 / A46472B): (*)

"It seems that Mr. Monro, over the last few days, has taken certain liberties without the Commissioner's consent, and ... refuses, in the future, to provide me with copies of his written or oral exchanges with the ministry. He regards my orders as a misinterpretation of his duties as Assistant Intelligence Commissioner. This declaration of independence from Mr. Monro is recent and I can not see why it is based.

The Police Commissioner is responsible for the criminal investigation department as for any other police department, but I can not perform my duties if an Assistant Commissioner proclaims his autonomy. I think that this conflict of authority jeopardizes, in the meantime, the security of the Capital and I defer to you to make it clear to Mr. Monro that as Assistant Commissioner; he must act entirely under the command of the Commissioner.

(*) The National Archives » de Kew: (HO 144/190 / A46472B)

James Monro hunts the ghost of Jack the Ripper

3

June 4, 1888
Monro meets Warren at Scotland Yard

When Warren's secretary entered the waiting room to tell Melville to come in, I slammed a firm hand on his chest and got up as quickly as possible. Melville looked at me with inquisitive amazement, restrained the upward movement, then leaned his back on the bench heavily, surprised.

"I'll meet him first, old man!" I said.

I already knew what was awaiting Melville Macnaghten between these four walls; he was going to be subjected to a mean spirited interrogation and defeated in advance. Warren continues to oppose this job offer. I did not want for anything in the world for this irritating character to prevent me from keeping my promise. I can not imagine the survival of my self-esteem in case of failure.

My friend travelled...to escape the Eastern life which had become intolerable to him.

I had witnessed his correspondence darken over the years.

It is imperative that I confront my enemy to honour this contract. With a nod, I made a sign to the secretary, I entered.

Warren is a long skinny figure and over his slender nose lays a pair of drooping glasses; like the main features of his face. Behind his desk, he was pasting a stamp on an envelope, and the vision of his brilliant tongue produced in me a reaction of deep disgust.

"There you are" he said; without straightening his head. From where I stood he looked like a tiny cricket.

The arrogance of luxury in which his office bathed only made him seem smaller. The bookshelves behind him were overloaded. His words flew away and disappeared into the large volume of his office.

"I have to talk to you, Mr Warren."

"That would be well, dear sir, but I must receive your Indian from one minute to the next."

"He will not come!"

The harsh tone of my voice does not accept any contradiction. He stopped pasting stamps, and raised two surprised round eyes in my direction.

He crossed his arms over his chest and tipped comfortably in his chair, like a big-bellied emir.

"Well! In that case what can I do for you Mr Monro?"

"I have come to talk to you about the one you call the Indian... I ask that you examine the candidacy of my respectable friend, Melville..."

"Stop right now! You bring this... Macnaghten into our headquarters, you have validated his arrival and his takeover of the entire service but you hid what happened in India!"

He said this with the air of a close friend who has just been betrayed, and the irony of his posture made him all the more detestable. I clenched my fists without saying anything.

"This is unworthy behaviour of a true gentleman, my dear Monro!"

His words were directed at me like a threatening sword. It was easy to understand the subtext: he was going to block his appointment!

"Sir! Macnaghten's candidacy is more than promoting a friend. We are talking about the grandson of the former governor, chief judge of Bengal, Francis Workman Macnaghten; whose son Elliot Macnaghten helped me find my footing in the Raj."

31

"Melville Leslie Macnaghten is a sturdy and serious character and his intellectual qualities fully justify his position. He is a person of great bravery, who has proved himself in India as elsewhere. So I testify before you and on my honour, that..."

"No, I couldn't care less about your friend's curriculum! You wanted to override your hierarchy Mr. Monro! I therefore oppose this appointment, using my right of veto."

I exploded.

"You... how dare you? He would be an asset for our police!"

Warren smiled. "Perhaps, but it is so ... It seems to me that your dear friend is not the immaculate knight you wish to portray ... I understand that his stay in India was far from peaceful. Remember this peasant revolt when they no longer wanted to pay Lord Ripon's royal taxes. That's how you met, did not you? Mr. Macnaghten is the only man in India to have been beaten by Hindus! So I cancelled this gentleman's appointment and I will not change my mind. "

I had acted as a beginner, relying exclusively on the influence of my position, and the certainty that this request would succeed.

I stood; standing in the room, the scornful look of Warren looked at me. The marble busts seemed to make fun of me. In the match of our rivalry, he had just scored a point.

"Your method is revolting!"

"You should have respected the hierarchy! Before entrusting a post of this importance, I missed absolutely some information on this Macnaghten..."

"Macnaghten is the man we need!"

"You do not doubt it, but I do not want it. He has no experience, and has never worked in the administration, either in London or in India, and moreover I learn that he has mistreated his employees!" He said casually that put me out of me.

For a few moments, an unpleasant silence invades the room. I clenched my teeth, holding back the violent words that hatred made me say. I controlled my rage, and with all my composure, I replied:

"Ah, that's it! Well, if you do not want to Melville Macnaghten; you will also do without my services. I will submit my resignation!"

Warren does not show any surprises.

"I'm waiting for your letter of resignation!"

I remained frozen; my eyes gave him a violent hatred.

"Your odious behaviour does not frighten me, Mr. Monro. You threaten me because you believe that your position within the yard will allow you to put pressure on my decision! Do not even think about it! I'll make you a revelation: I also propose my resignation! That surprises you, does not it? He said to me with aplomb. Relative to the situation, Secretary Henry Matthews will have no choice but to validate your request, rather than lose me ... He is a very good friend. What do you think about this? You do not answer? In this case, you can have Mr. Monro and by the way; take your Indian friend, do you want to?"

"Bastard damn wicked Welsh!" I mumbled out of the office.

Seeing me Melville got up.

"James is you all right?"

"Certainly not! This carne Warren has lived up to its reputation!"

"James what does that mean?"

"I'm afraid you can not work with us... At least for now!"

I do not have the courage to add that the chief commissioner has thrown our hopes into the sea Melville whines.

As usual, he was perfectly calm, but from all the pores of his skin, and from all the openings of his body, came a breath of dissatisfaction such that the guilt that squeezed my throat was transformed into a real shame.

"Melville ... I ... am sincerely ... sorry. I was certain ... that I will get his turn in your presence. It's my fault... I have sinned out of pride. But the more I confused myself in excuses, the more I sank into the quicksands of embarrassment. Something in my friend's gaze became cold and lifeless."

"If I can offer you a little consolation, know that I will immediately resign!" (*)

"It's quite worthy of you, James. You are loyal whatever happens."

"We have nothing left to do here, my dear fellow. We should think about an alternative for you! We will find a solution!"

A few steps further ... "How about a little ginger beer?"

He smiles weakly despite his deep disappointment.

(*) Evening News London, U.K. September 5, 1888 The disputes between Sir Charles Warren and Mr. Monro arose out of statements.... Sir Charles Warren withdrew his recommendations,

The next day Tuesday, June 5, 1888 Melville Macnaghten sends the following letter (HO 144/190 / A46472B):

London 9 Tite Street

Mr. Minister, with regard to my appointment as assistant chief, whose request was made by Mr. Monro on March 17, and approved by Sir Charles Warren on March 19, sanctioned by yourself on March 29, 1888, I please tell me why unexplained, my assignment has not been published. I was kept on hold and unemployed for the past two months...

I believe that this appointment may be published immediately, unless satisfactory reasons for its cancellation can be attributed to me.

I have the honour to be, Sir, your most obedient servant.

Signed; Melville Macnaghten. (*)

June 7 Melville Macnaghten is made aware by a letter from Minister Henri Matthews that his appointment has been denied by Charles Warren.

On June 11, I write to Under-Secretary of State Minister Godfrey Lushington Under-Secretary of State at the Ministry (HO 144/190 / A46472B)"I send this official letter with regret, but the state of affairs leaves me no option.

(*) The National Archives » de Kew: (HO 144/190 / A46472B)

In view of the actions taken by Sir Charles Warren to peddle slanders about me, and to question my integrity, I consider myself entitled to request that I be provided with the elements that would justify such accusations, and that conduct a proper inquiry into the matter. Regardless of the personal propensities that bind me to this case, it is my duty to point out that the problem that has been raised goes far beyond simply assigning a post from assistant to chief of police. The accusations of Sir Charles Warren are based on the totally erroneous interpretation of my duties as assistant commissioner in charge of intelligence. In 1884 I was selected and appointed to the head of the department by the Secretary of State, and I performed these functions more successfully than my predecessor. In addition, I renounced a high office in the administration of Her Majesty the Queen for this position.

The functioning of the intelligence department, inaugurated since 1878, has never ceased to function thus, with the blessing of the various secretaries of state to succeed one another. The makeovers of Sir Charles Warren pervert the existing mode of operation, namely that the Intelligence is under the exclusive authority of the officer in charge of it, and returns to the procedures of yesteryear, procedures condemned by the commission.

The result of these manoeuvres is already visible. This change will certainly have serious consequences. As long as this problem is not solved, the intelligence department can not function properly, and these new restrictions force me to declare myself not responsible for the possible bad results that this service could produce. I solemnly declare that the accusations of Sir Charles Warren, concerning the administration of the department, or of myself, must be the subject of a complete examination by a competent authority, knowing that it is urgent to treat the question, in view of its impact on the general interest".

(On June 20, the Secretary of State will reject the investigation.) Sir Charles Warren will think that Monro is once again trying to override his control, and will now call this conflict of authority a crisis.)

On July 24, from James Monro to Sir Charles Warren (MEPO 4/487):

"I was sent to town today by the Secretary of State. I wanted to go back to the office, but I was unable to do it. My health does not allow me to work, so I wish you to leave me the rest of the week, after which I propose to take my usual leave of the month of August".

On the same day Sir Charles Warren wrote to James Monro (MEPO 4/487):

I'm sorry to hear you're sick. You can, as you propose, take leave until the end of August and I will arrange for your duties during this period to be assigned to another Assistant Commissioner (*)

On August 17, 1888, I wrote the following letter to the Ministry: (HO 144/190 / A46472C).

Sir it is with great regret that I feel compelled to postpone my resignation from the office of the Assistant Commissioner, Metropolitan Police, in charge of the Criminal Investigation Department. There have been serious differences of opinion on the questions of the administration of the police between Sir Charles Warren and myself, and I feel that under a change of policy and system, which my long experience compels me to withdraw; I can not continue my mission for the efficiency of the criminal investigation department, which was specially entrusted to me by the Secretary of State in 1884 " I therefore resign, which is accepted by Godfrey Lushington on behalf of the Home Secretary on August 21, and I officially leave my office on August 31, 1888.

(*) Days of my Years – Melville Macnaghten 1914 p 50

James Monro hunts the ghost of Jack the Ripper

4
Saturday, August 4, 1888
Lyceum Theatre; Dr Jekyll & Mister Hide

As we drove down in the cab, we passed the baroque columns that support the facade of the venerable theatre; which looks like an ancient temple.

Away from the capital for seven years, Melville was amazed by this wonder. My young friend opened his mouth and eyes wide while we were queuing with the people of the world.

To see this serious thirty-five-year-old hunter showing the same face as a child in a toy store is a little pleasure.

"Sumptuous!"

"Is it not?"

"There is a crazy world" he said; turning his head from left to right.

"Yes, this representation is very successful; I think that the two thousand places are reserved."

Melville was aware of the quality of the event, superb in his evening dress.

The opener took our tickets and led us through the lobby to the balcony, by white marble stairs.

"Look at this splendour that the management of this gentleman Irving has given!"

"I agree with you!"

"You will see the living room. It's as big as the lobby!"

It is lined with noble woods, period engravings, sculptures of Athena, Apollo, Aphrodite, and Dionysus. We were seated on comfortable armchairs. The air shook with the excitement of the upcoming show, and our view of the stage was breathtaking.

Burgundy velvet curtains stretched on both sides of the stage, others framed the royal boxes.

"Have you ever seen Richard Mansfield play?" Melville asked me.

"No, but friends have seen the rehearsals, and they told me he's amazing. The light effects are sensational!"

"I'm looking forward to it."

In a continuous buzz the spectators took their seats, like bees in a hive and we enjoyed watching them.

"I am saddened by this debacle concerning the position I proposed to you my friend!"

"Oh! Do not worry about my fate James; I'm busy importing tea from Bengal. And I am very happy."

"Are you telling the truth?"

"Absolutely my dear. It turns out that following your advice, I also came to London to escape the deleterious atmosphere that reigns in Bombay right now. You were right in view of the latest news! I do not hide that my wife is relieved to leave this hostile country. Obviously, the prospect of your promise has precipitated our departure, but you know me James, I can not go hunting without keeping some spare cartridges, in case the animal is tougher than expected, am I not right?"

I never take a decision without taking all eventualities into account. In case your promise can not be kept, I already knew that I could count on my father to find me a job, which allowed me to keep my status as head of the family.

I encourage him to reveal to me the nature of the other job he had in mind.

"Thanks to my father Elliot's relationship; I work at Kearley & Tonge importing tea from Kishnaghur property." (*)

He looked a little disappointed by this blow of fate, but he kept a good countenance.

"By Jupiter, it's splendid," I told him rubbing his shoulder vigorously. Under his blonde moustache; I saw a little shy smile. I laughed at his school boyish embarrassment.

"Dora did not want to come?"

Melville became gloomy and answered hesitantly:

"She is in no mood to go out tonight... She prefers the house and the company of children. It's their birthday soon!"

"What a pity, I do not have the pleasure to admire the beautiful face of the charming Dora ... You are a lucky one, I tell him by nudging him nicely; you captured a beautiful creature."

(*) Melville is hired at "Kearley and Tonge" (Miter Square).

"Have you heard of those horrible crimes in Whitechapel?" Melville asked to change the subject, looking up from his program.

"Yes in April a woman named Emma Smith, was assaulted and died the next day at the London Hospital. These murders of prostitutes are becoming more numerous."

"Ah? Melville's eye lit up."

I see Warren's mess. Melville has all the postures of the hound. I decided to clarify the situation, to satisfy the professional curiosity of my friend.

"There are so many murders in the Whitechapel neighbourhood, and so few arrests!"

I realized that I was talking about atrocious passions, in a place crowded with honest people, but the general hubbub was a real barrier around us, like the invisible walls of a small private office. I moved closer to his ear.

"The press keep on harping about every murder to keep discrediting the effectiveness of our police. It is enough for several prostitutes to die in less than a year, so that journalists immediately think of a single killer."

We interrupted our conversion, for an imposing gentleman in a velvet frock coat, top hat and cane in his hand, passed in the row, apologizing loudly.

(*) April 3, Emma Smith was assaulted, at the corner of Osborn Street

At the same times, the light in the theatre dimmed, the play was about to begin. I motioned to Melville that I would pursue the conversation during the interlude. The theatre was plunged into darkness, and immediately the silence came. Only the scene remained slightly illuminated. In silence the curtain rose on a laboratory provided with stills and twisted glass pipes. Jars filled with colourful products were placed on large shelves. Although the place revealed a chemistry laboratory, it was difficult to compare it with anything other than the medieval workshop of an alchemist. A worm-eaten doorbell rattled in the room. Mansfield appeared dressed in a green blouse and flannel trousers. He moved delicately, examined some jars, and played taps. The still was whistling and producing a thick vapour which was heard in the midst of the muteness of the intrigued spectators. At the end of a twisted circuit, a vial was filled drop by drop with a fluorescent yellow liquid. Making sure of the proper handling, the doctor expressed a concentrated look of enthusiastic intelligence. He made the flame burn with a benzene beak and paused. He turned to the audience and declared:

"My work on the human soul is reaching its goal. Thanks to my experiences and my chemical knowledge, I will be able to dissociate the honest part of the human spirit from its vicious part.

This scourge worse than the plague which walks in our streets and flows in our blood. This miraculous potion will allow us to isolate Evil for the good of humanity!"

He grabbed the vial and swallowed the contents. Suddenly Jekyll / Mansfield complained of grimacing pains, and suddenly a thunderclap broke out in the hall, surprising the audience. Multicoloured light effects streak the darkness as the actor's transformation continues. Mansfield was amazing. He foamed and groaned, pulling on his collar furiously his features deformed horribly, subject to the inevitable molecular metamorphosis that took place in him. He collapsed violently on the floor, in front of the horrified audience. The public remained astonished, as in the face of a terrible catastrophe.

The lady sitting next to me seemed to faint, I gently pushed her away from my arm. I glanced at Melville: he looked like a hound dog in front of an exceptional game. I saw the raised edges of his blond moustache tremble, his pupils studying the scene with the precision of an archer. His eyes followed every movement of the actor, every change of his face. I did not dare disturb him in this intense moment; but I could not help but be frightened at him. The scene, and most importantly, Richard Mansfield's play, seemed to penetrate him to the very depths of his body.

The actor continued to dissect the human soul with the precision of a surgeon. He brought out the darkest areas of our forbidden desires. Melville stiffened in his chair, all his senses awake, but dumb as a grave. At intermission finally he said:

"A remarkable interpretation!"

A glass of ginger beer in his hand, Melville looked like an Athenian god. The play was a great success; it was enough to observe the crowd all around us. I see enough Evil day after day, to understand this transformation of Dr. Jekyll into a filthy Mister Hide! I said.

Melville took another sip from his drink.

"I must say that Mansfield is admirable. Do you realize all of this is hardly due to make up? A wig, a moustache, and a simple play of light, and here we are with a new man, what am I saying, an atrocious monster!"

"I see you're excited about comedy, my dear, that's nice to see."

"Alas! He said with a tone of great sadness. If only my father had not stopped me from becoming a theatre actor!"

He gave me a sickly smile, and I could see the nostalgia and disappointment in his eyes.

"Hey there, my friend, do not be so peeved; if you'll allow me that word. Your father entrusted you with this important plantation in India." I immediately felt I had touché a score point.

"You have managed a perfect marriage, with wonderful children! "

You still have not told me how your beautiful wife is?

"I prefer not to talk about that!"

Once again my attempt to divert the conversation had been disastrous. His eyes froze, revealing the internal tension of his couple.

"Excuse me; I lack tact!"

"No, not at all!" he said in a suddenly lighter tone. "Do not worries about my reaction, your attitude prove that you are a good friend and I thank you for it. Let's change the subject, simply. Have you read Robert Louis Stevenson's book?"

"My work leaves me little time."

"I understand that with the many recent crimes you have to deal with."

"Oh yes! It seems that these assassins are elusive, that they do not exist."

"Hem ... We could almost call them Nemo" Suggested Melville.

"I beg your pardon?"

"Nemo means nobody in Latin. Did you not read that novel by that French writer called - Twenty thousand leagues under the sea - in 1870?"

"Now that you mention it, it rings a bell.

Jules Verne isn't it?"

My friend's face lit up immediately.

"That's right! You see that you have time to read."

"At the time, I did but now we are overwhelmed, with Charles Warren's refusal, the problems in the district of Whitechapel and these prostitute murders!"

The bell rang to recall us back into our seats. We quickly regained our seats in the rustle of dresses and frock coats, leaving the bar and the golden chandeliers ... The play resumed with the spectacle of a man tortured by his demons. At the end of the performance a row of applause flooded the room in honour of Richard Mansfield who humbly greeted the jubilant audience. Melville stood up to applaud; his gaze was subdued by the awesome actor. In an indescribable hubbub, we headed for the exit.

"Oh! James, my friend, do not hail a cab. Let's walk a little; I'd like to take a few steps, in a calm place."

"As you wish, Melville, a little walk will not hurt me."

We walked slowly towards Waterloo Bridge, moving away from the festive lights. The cabs scampered from all directions towards the Lyceum, to accompany the spectators. The night was soft and calm. The clatter of our soles and the rattling of our canes beat the measure of our footsteps.

"Silence, darkness, this is an atmosphere that pleases me."

"You are thoughtful tonight, my dear Melville."

"I think this show has awakened the double personality that lies dormant in me."

"Artist, I do not doubt it, you would certainly be a good policeman! I'm sure!"

Melville looked at me with some confusion.

"I do not despair of you entering the Yard. This refusal with Warren is only a setback. He has been on the hot seat since "The Bloody Sunday". Recent murders are frightening the press and the public. The people are a kind of enormous creature, guided by an intractable conscience. It does not matter to him to know the culprit; the people want to bring down the highest ranking officer. For us policemen, it will be necessary to unravel these knots, so that the public does not let loose against them. We have a great responsibility that does not tolerate incompetence. Our leader Warren is bad and inconsistent. "

"In a short time, I guarantee you those newspapers will make a fortune. Warren will be strongly criticized, which is not displeasing me. It seems that the whole district of the London Hospital is infected with gangs of thieves who flee in broad daylight with impunity."

"If my instinct is not wrong, Warren will have to resign in a short time, and I'll get you back to the Yard at that moment."

Melville said nothing. He seemed to light up like a weak fire.

"James, thank you, this setback is unfortunate, certainly, but I will focus on my work at Kearley & Tonge. You know, I can not tell you that my life was horrible! I have good memories of my studies at Eton College."

We had passed Waterloo Station when he resumed.

"My wife Dora is a woman of fine intelligence. Our relations though cordial are no longer very warm at this moment, do you understand me?"

I nodded. Good manners forbade him to express himself crudely. His distress was shared by thousands of British husbands, their couple's sex life was floundering and half-heartedly he explained to me that he no longer had sex with his wife.

"Has it been a long time?"

"Yes!"

I kept quiet to allow him to express himself freely.

"At first everything was fine. The births of Charles Melville and Julia Mary were a divine blessing. I loved my wife intensely. No clouds passed in our radiant sky. Seven years ago, in May 1881, there was this accident that changed my life! My God ... I constantly remember that. When I went to the village to explain myself with the rebels who did not want to pay their taxes, I was with my employees. The farmers had come out of their huts to listen to me. I do not know what happened, the spokesperson assaulted me and hit me so hard with a stick on the side of his head that I fell unconscious. All this not to pay the royal taxes of Lord Ripon! I was in a coma, and it was as if I had made a trip to the afterlife."

He looked at me sadly, trying to minimize this trauma with this little joke about this trip from beyond the grave. This event must have been too upsetting. I did not dare to speak. I cursed my poor rhetorical talents, and let the harsh London with blow. It was a good ides, he confessed again a little more.

"Since then I have to tell you that it's not exactly the same with Dora, as if the bond between us was broken.

A strange icy feeling took hold of me and has never left me for seven years."

"Something invisible stalks me and keeps me hostage.

I fell like a prey." (*)

"Melville you must not let yourself down. I understand that such a trauma must be difficult to overcome. I do not doubt for a moment that you will overcome this. Do not worry about Dora, the homecoming will be good for your couple and new kids will come soon to brighten your home. Dora will wait; it's only been seven years without a new birth, right?"

Melville was silent. His eyes expressed a "if you say so" that did not require additional words. Charles Warren pushed me to resign which will do at the end of my holiday in August.

Suddenly Melville signalled to a cab that was passing by.

"Let's go back now, shall we?"

Melville gave the destination; 9 Tite Street; the coachman immediately whipped the horses.

"I'll leave the cab once you arrive, you'll forgive me, and I feel tired. This evening has worn me out. It's as if Richard Mansfield had introduced me to a mirror."

On the way back I saw his pallor increase.

(*) Days of my Years - Melville Macnaghten 1914 p 51

James Monro hunts the ghost of Jack the Ripper

Since we left the theatre I could not help but notice his desire to get away from the world, and he seemed to be immersed in his thoughts, despite, or because of, our discussion. Dr. Jekyll and Mr. Hyde stirred some dark memories in Melville, and I told myself that he probably did not confide his secret to many other people. Moments later, the cab stopped at 9 Tite Street in front of the beautiful 3-story red brick house; which had an imposing first floor balcony. (1)

He went down and paid the coachman. I grabbed his hand through the cab window.

"I beg you, hold on, my friend, do you promise?"

He turned his head towards me, with a slight smile, climbed the few steps and pushed open the large glass door of the entrance. I gave my address to the coachman for my return home. (2)

(1) Kew Archives, Melville Macnaghten lives at 9 Tite Street.
His friend Oscar Wilde lives at 34 Tite Street.

(2) Kew Archives: on August 21, 1888, James Monro resigned, which was immediately accepted by Godfrey Lushington on behalf of the Home Secretary, with effect from August 28, 1888.
James Monro officially leaves his office on August 30, 1888

James Monro hunts the ghost of Jack the Ripper

5

Thursday, August 30, 1888, Shadwell; District of Whitechapel

That evening a beautiful moon illuminated without distinction the wealthy and miserable neighbourhoods of London. The pollution of the atmosphere was imprinted on the skin of the walker, with the limited vision, in the chiaroscuro generated by the street lamps. The mist overflowed the quays like a witch's cauldron and stuck to the hulls of the ships lined up in the London docks.

A long silhouette stood out in the fog. The pace of his step showed the strongest determination. Without difficulty he slipped like an eel gliding along the walls, to the large basin of the dry dock at Ratcliff. An imposing ship with three masts occupied most of the pit, and in a red letter it was possible to read on the stern; *The Connovia*.

The figure climbed aboard the ship and pulled out a bottle of alcohol from his black mass, which he methodically dumped on folded cotton sails in an opening of the bridge.

He scratched a match; the space of the ignition revealing the face of a man. He threw the burning toothpick on the soaked sails. Immediately an impressive blue flame rose along the mast. The gaze of the man savoured for a moment that nascent blaze. Then he jumped onto the wharf, heading for the southern part of the Shadwell Docks Whitechapel District. The man walked along the warehouses and stopped in front of the sign:

"WAREHOUSE OF THE COMPANY OF INDIA"

"Elliot Macnaghten"

A simple steel chain closed the door. He pulled out an iron bar from his coat and levered the padlock. The metal gave way like a string, and fell to the ground with a tingle amplified by the silence of the night. The shadow entered and looked at the crates that were piling up from floor to ceiling. They contained bottles of Gin and Brandy, propped up by straw. The hand rubbed the rough wood with his gloved fingers. He knocked over a box, which vomited glass and alcohol in a din of broken crockery. He scratched a new match, and threw it on the puddle of alcohol. A blue wave swept over the straw reserve. He flew quickly to the docks unseen. A few hundred yards away, he stopped to contemplate the fire.

The British Venice flared up like a 1666 engravings. The night streaked with orange-red lit the docks. A few moments later, the bells of the fire cars, pulled by imposing horses, were heard. A monstrous horse spitting steam by the nostrils rushed into the fog pulling a heavy pump. It was followed by a van loaded with men and pipes, followed by a troop of helmeted men, armed with axes. One of them, mounted on a muscular steed, repelled the passers by who had began to gather on the quays. The hippo mobiles were put in place and the pipes were deployed. These state of the art machines were casting life saving water at heights never seen before. Only two servicemen operated this pump, when once a long human chain of buckets would not have been enough to extinguish the fire. An unbearable heat prevailed on the docks. Fire fighters were using all their might to stem the onslaught of flames that had begun to nibble the nearby warehouses. The memory of the great London fire reinforced the fireman's determination. On the tinted mirror of the Thames we could discern the outlines of the pump boats; carpet like toads; spitting rain on the ember monster. Hundreds of colonial goods were charred; several nearby warehouses were also destroyed; the magnificent *"The Connovia"* was dying.

Around eleven o'clock, the fire-fighters managed to limit the progression of the fire. The curls of smoke were still escaping from the charred ruins. (*)

Mary Ann Nichols, also nicknamed Polly, was a small woman looking like a doll. She was coming back from the show offered by the fireman. That night, she was wearing a brand new black hat. At the corner of Osborn Street and Whitechapel Road, Polly met Emily Holland who was leaving the grocer's. Emily seemed worried to see her friend staggering. The church clock struck two thirty in the morning. Polly reassured her; she was looking for a man with a few pennies in his pocket to finish the night. Sixpence is the price she asked the sailor in the middle of Withechapel Road. Of course he accepted; and the couple walked by the squalid and sordid side of Buck's Row to a stable barn. The man with the dark cloth cap could not see the sadness engraved on Polly's face. The run down buildings of Whitechapel did not look like decent dwellings. She was walking between two tight walls that were getting closer, hugging her, choking her. Her trachea crashed, and she did not have time to make a noise. The strangler mastered his gesture perfectly. With his red scarf he exerted a fatal pressure on her small frame.

* London Advertiser (September 1, 1888).

Polly struggled noiselessly; in vain. When she was soft; he laid her gently on the ground. The blade of his kukri slashed her throat, and very little blood ran down the left side of her neck. The shreds of her conscience felt the blade sinking into the flesh of her belly. Four strikes opened her stomach from the sternum to the pelvis. Polly's soul had left her body, leaving only her empty flesh to the murderer. The assassin cleaned the strange curved weapon with Polly's clothes and slipped it into his leather bag. (*)

Mary Ann Nichols le 31 août 1888 Bucks Row

He turned back, crossed Thomas Street; and slid his key into the big door of the Kearley & Co warehouse. He hurried up to the second floor of the building and entered his office.

(*) PALL MALL GAZETTE SATURDAY, SEPTEMBER 1, 1888

Jack undressed, washed the blood and the iron taste that stained his person. He bartered his old rags for clothes that betrayed his belonging to the upper caste. He quickly took out his pocket watch, it indicated 3:30 in the morning; the street was deserted.

He locked the door, turned to Borth Street and walked to the empty hall of Whitechapel and Mile End Station. The small shopkeepers and workmen had begun to go out, greeting the new day and set up their stalls. Others left to work with a heavy and resigned pace. His train was starting quickly towards Westminster. The man entered his spacious living room. He opened the buffet and poured himself a glass of gin. The red berry taste; tingled his tongue. Through the window he saw the incipient light flood the street.

6
Saturday, September 8th 1888
Hanbury Street; Whitechapel

Dark Annie was taciturn. It was just one of many nicknames; but it was the one that suited her best. Her eyebrows fell heavily on her piercing eyes, and her pale face under her jet black hair gave her a serious look. Dark Annie ... A succession of misfortunes, missteps had made her fall from servant in Windsor to the disgusting sidewalks of this other part of London. Dark Annie was still wearing dark clothes, the last signs of an old chaste life, now she was prostituting herself. When Jack approached, she raised her eyes to him. He was a tall stature that stood above her head.

Far from the rowdy voices coming from the pubs, she led him through a door, at number twenty-nine Hanbury Street; into an infamous backyard separated from the neighbouring gardens by a fence among the weeds.

She had not yet stuck to the planks of wood when a piece of cloth tightened around her throat.

29 Hanbury Street

"Nooo ... "She moaned.

The splinters stuck in his cheek when her head slid against the wood. Rusty and wet nails became wicked poisonous hooks. The hard heavy palm of her assailant pressed on her terrified face, deforming it. When the adrenaline from her brain overcame the terrible pain, she felt as if she was snatched into nothingness; her trachea was crushing, her mouth was writhing. Three minutes later the red scarf, escaping from Jack's hand; allowed his prey to slip smoothly against the palisade. He took out his kukri brought back from Calcutta.

With an assured gesture, he opened poor Annie's throat like that of a hunted animal and with an ample movement, cut her neck right to the spine.

The blood was squirting against the boards. This sad puppet of flesh who could note utter a last word was sprawled in the mud. He cut the muscle ties. He snapped them apart. In his sticky hands, he pushed back the shining guts. Jack was no longer in a London backyard but back in the undergrowth of the Burmese jungle. The beast slipped his hands among the hot offal. The bowels made trivial sounds of sucking and flatulence, he placed them on Dark Annie's shoulder. Kneeling, Jack busied himself with Annie's crotch. He cut the genitals, to clear part of the bladder and especially the uterus. He took them with the delicacy reserved for precious giblets and slipped them into a canvas bag. He removed the brass rings from Annie's finger; a fancy derisory of three rings, and placed it on the floor with all the contents of her pockets. Jack got up and went out quickly into the street. He walked briskly and hurried on Hanbury Street. Turning left he was running down Osborn Street to Whitechapel Road. He entered the Kearley & Tonge building at Mitre Square. The guard was absent, as every Saturday night.

He locked himself upstairs in his office, placed his trophy in a jar filled with alcohol, and reserved a special jar for the uterus. It fascinated him; his sick mind ordered him to devour this feminine symbol, a delectation he reserved for later. He washed his stained hands, took off his sailor's disguise, and carefully put it away in his locked closet. Dawn was rising Jack come out the front door, which he took care to lock. He boarded the Whitechapel District Railway train which took him home to Westminster. In his living room, he was shocked by the contrast between the serene calm of his opulent home, and the excitement that was to reign somewhere in a small, shabby little garden in a squalid Whitechapel street. (*)

(*) PALL MALL GAZETTE, SATURDAY, SEPTEMBER 8, 1888.

7
September 11, 1888
Monro meets Abberline at Scotland Yard

After my August vacation, my resignation was accepted on August 21st, with effect from August 28th. Henry Matthews had appointed me head of the intelligence department, with the mission of working closely with the ministry's officials, without Charles Warren's knowledge.

In the late morning, I met Frederick Abberline, dragging his feet in the corridors. I greeted him and he stood still. The inspector answered me.

"Hello, Commissioner Monro!" He whispered.

"Abberline, you have a compassionate mine!"

"Do not talk to me about it..."

Abberline displayed his thick sideburns as usual. On his skull his baldness seemed to have appropriated more space. His eyes were hollow with rings of fatigue. His drawn features made him look older, making him look like an anaemic old beggar.

"Looks like all the London lights are up." I was on my way to my office.

"Very well, inspector, let's go, you will summarize the situation."

"Oh it's such a tricky situation. If you care to accompany me!"

I followed Abberline who like a shield dismissed the hordes of uniformed policemen swarming down the corridor; like busy ants.

"All this has neither head nor tail! To begin with, in the spring, April 3, Emma Smith was fatally wounded, by a group of young people, everything followed very quickly then. There was the murder of Martha Tabram on August 7th. Thirty nine bayonet stab wounds ... Thirty-nine!"

"It was still in Whitechapel, wasn't it?"

"George Yard to be precise, another prostitute. Then on August 30, the fire at Shadwell Docks; immediately followed by the murder of Mary Ann Nichols!"

"Two problems in one night. To see things on the bright side, our fire fighters are brave; they were able to extinguish the flames. Alas! It was too late for poor Marie Ann. Her friend Emily Holland testified that she saw Mary Ann Nichols at the corner of Withechapel Road and Osborn Street at two thirty in the morning. This is the last person to have seen her alive."

Nichol's corpse is found an hour later in the deserted Buck's Row; 100 meters from the Kearley & Co building. A certain Charles Cross fell on the horror, early in the morning around three forty. He picked up an agent, but PC John Neil had arrived first from the north. By the light of his lantern he had seen Nichols lying on the ground. The dress was raised, and as the fellow was prudish, he had pulled the garments over her legs. They had not realised the hubris.

"PC John Neil has responded well."

"Later we had the gentlemen of L & P Walter & Son who went to write to our dear Minister Matthews to give a sum of money to help stop the murderer. All the press thinks that these three crimes are related, in particular the Star newspaper!"

"Yes, but the reward request has been refused."

"It's just that this kind of initiative hurts me. Citizens believe they are doing better than the police and can restore order more effectively. These rewards lead to too many false testimonies"

"You are preaching to a convert!"

My answer snatched a smile from Abberline; he told me he regretted my resignation.

I replied that I could not go back on my decision and besides I did not regret it Robert Anderson would do the job perfectly; after his rest in Switzerland.

"I respect your choice, sir, but we must recognize that it is a loss for us."

"It sounds like you're talking about a dead man; Abberline! You see too much right now!"

"It is the least we can say!"

"I know that these three cases have nothing in common. Inspector Helson finally conceded that there was no evidence linking these murders to each other. This has been said. Do not worry about the past. We must go ahead; we must keep the hacks of the Star newspaper at bay."

"I can not contradict you, sir."

We arrived in front of his office. He opened the door. The room was cluttered with files, reports, papers scattered everywhere.

"I do not dare to ask you if the same mess is in your house.

"Oh! Sir no! I assure you all these are old files." He says dismissing papers. The last case ... here!"

Abberline was able to find all the files in this clutter; He retrieved a file from the top of a pile and opened it.

"September 8 ... A woman is found dead at twenty-nine Hanbury Street."

I sat on a chair without asking permission.

"Well, I'm listening to you. Do not hesitate to remind me precisely of all the details."

"A Sir John Richardson, thirty-seven years old (Abberline conscientiously read his sheets); says that he entered the courtyard of twenty-nine Hanbury Street, to check the padlock on the door of the cellar of his mother's worshop. At a quarter to five in the morning, he stayed there for a moment to repair his boot."

"Let's admit you can skip this kind of information."

"Forgive me Chief. I'm just repeating what the evidence says."

"In this case ... Continue."

"So he did not notice anything unusual. At about twenty past twenty; that is at the hour of the crime, we have Mr Albert Cadosch, twenty-seven years old, residing at twenty-seven Hanbury Street; who declares he heard a voice uttering a feeble "Nooo"; on the other side of the fence that separates the two gardens. A few minutes later, coming back from the toilet at the back of his backyard; he heard the sound; I quote, "of a body slipping along the fence."

"And the crime?"

Just a minute!"

He stops reading. His look becomes sharp. It was the bloodhound who was following his trail.

The dead woman was found thirty minutes after Cadosch had heard these noises. It was a man named John Davis who found the body. A misplaced show, at this time of day!

"Moved at any time! I remind you that a few days before, on September 5, we were treated to this ugly joke from the newspaper Star!"

"They hurried to convict a suspect, remember?"

"Very good."

"John Pfizer, also nicknamed Leather Apron ! Ah! We can say that they went quickly to work. I'm sure they did not blush when we cleared him... Case closed, unsolved!"

No gentleman from the newspaper ever wrote an article to apologise. One would think they could move on to more serious things?

We looked at each other while walking. We knew how rushed the journalists are as soon as they find a news item dirty enough to tell. These low level Stevenson's, who thought themselves the literary elite, were only good enough to make the concierges shudder in their boxes. Whitechapel is full of crimes, and we were constantly overwhelmed."

"I realize that I made you come for little; you will understand that in light of recent events. This latest murder is not going to improve the situation. Journalists will be unleashed in a few hours; I needed to expose the situation to an experienced man like you."

"I appreciate your compliments; Abberline, and you're right; we'll have to keep a cool head. The scribblers will be the first to make easy shortcuts, and we have the city to hold. The slightest spark could trigger a fire in Whitechapel. Stay on the lookout for new developments and conduct your investigation like the captain of a ship in a stormy sea. Avoid the pitfalls, concentrate on each case, I do not need to teach you anything. The press will continue to link everything into one and the same assassin; we know that this is false. The last two murders have nothing to do with the previous two. The crowds enjoy the sensational concept of a single bogeyman."

"Do not be swayed. In my eyes; you seem to be down to earth, inspector. Keep this attitude."

"Thank you sir!"

"Perfect. I will have to go. Good luck Abberline and keep me informed of any discovery you make, do you want to?"

"Very well sir!" I said.

I took leave of the inspector, leaving him in the middle of his chaos.

* Daily News United Kingdom 10 September 1888

James Monro hunts the ghost of Jack the Ripper

8
Friday, September 28, 1888
Athenaeum Club Pall Mall

A marble Apollo watched the entrance to the club, above the main staircase. Some gentlemen circulated here and there, taking off or putting on their coats. It was a quiet hour. I put my overcoat on the butler. Under a marble sculpture, I saw Melville's tall figure. As usual, he had a splendid posture, an aristocratic elegance. His blond moustache rose on either side of his face in a placid double curve, he took my hand firmly, his face still expressed, but in a more discreet way, the strange melancholy he had shown me after the Lyceum show.

"James!"

"Melville ... You have competition above you!" (*)

He turned his head to look at the statue behind him.

"A famous member. This club has a very strict policy."

"How are you, dear friend?"

"Well. Can I offer you a beer?"

"Thanks!"

"Follow me!"

(*) https://fr.wikipedia.org/wiki/Club_Athenaeum

Through long corridors; an alignment of statues gave a successful imitation of an antique decor. We joined the salon; following a superb frieze imitation of the Parthenon. a thick carpet with floral motives absorbed the noise transmitted by our polished shoes. We took a seat in deep and rich armchairs. Once installed, another butler asked us with extreme politeness, what we wanted to consume. Melville asked for a ginger beer; adding that he would like some newspapers of the day. The butler bent and turned around. He returned with a tray with two glasses of beer and a bundle of magazines. My friend picked one.

"The Morning Advertiser and The Star of September 28th; there are plenty of details about the latest murder" he said waving them.

"I did not think I told you that much. It's a mistake to talk to George Sims about this. He is a nice character, but he takes his job too much to heart." (*)

"My friend Sims? Oh! I did not tell him anything! I see that his colleagues have no trouble producing lines without my help!"

"All I notice is that there are two ideas that keep coming up in these articles: Charles Warren's resignation and ineffective policing."

(*) https://fr.wikipedia.org/wiki/George_Robert_Sims

I deliberately omit the lines of bloody details and irrelevant information.

"It does not help the Yard, Melville!"

"You do not beat around the bush! For your information I learnt details in those articles. I keep abreast of all recent events. You are an informant of choice."

I felt Melville was in a teasing, almost mischievous mood. No wonder this paradox; those unresolved riddles allowed many people to play amateur detectives, mostly around a pint of beer, or a glass of Brandy.

I felt pity for Abberline forced to struggle between meagre clues and popular delusions.

"I read that the inquest for the murder of the last victim, who was identified as "Annie Chapman", opened on September 10. This woman, Mrs. Long, says that she saw a man talking with her shortly before her death."

"You made a good inquiry."

"Yes. This story is fascinating!"

"Fascinating? Disgusting perhaps; horrible surely; madness is the exact term. Londoners are scared, and we know what fear can do to men"

"By the way, who is this George Lusk?"

He was appointed leader of TheWhitechapel Vigilante Committee on September 10.

"Indeed he is an entrepreneur who works on the decoration of auditoriums and restaurants. Rich Jewish businessmen from Whitechapel appointed him to head their vigilance committee. Their treasurer, Joseph Aarons, had written to the Daily Telegraph asking Secretary Matthews to offer a reward for capturing the murderer of these poor women." (*)

"I have read also that Sir Montagu has proposed a reward of one hundred pound."

"It's an important reward!"

"The ministry refused. He is drowning under these kinds of requests."

"I do want to believe you. Newspapers do not help. You have already stopped several « Nemo », and none was the right one. Pizer the leather apron; then Isenschmid the butcher ... Crazy it seems!"

"A good suspect indeed. But there is no proof of his guilt."

"Oh! The optogram? Is it possible that Chapman's retina could have engraved the killer's image on its surface?"

Melville jumped from one idea to another, all his sentences referred to the murders and the inquest. He was excited and impatient like a toddler in a circus show.

(*) https://en.wikipedia.org/wiki/George_Lusk

"Unthinkable! It is a fabulous of the Star. A theory proposed by so-called scientists based on an experiment on rabbits."

"I did not think you were so credulous, my good friend. Nowadays, scientists believe that they hold the key to all mysteries; I think they are going too fast. A bit too extravagant this optogram story." (*)

This is the kind of sensational news, halfway between the police investigation and the six pennies catalogues. Melville was swinging back in his seat, and fixing the ceiling with a look of nostalgia; he said smiling:

"I loved these magazines."

"I remember it very well!" I said.

We looked at each other with the complicity of two old friends. I remembered all these miscellaneous facts, all these murderers about which Melville was inexhaustible: the usher James Blomfield Rusch became a murderer, Marie Manning hanged for murdering her lover, the murder of Lord William Russel by Courvoisier; the prince of poison.

Morbid fantasies, but childish, that he had narrated to me when we had met there in India.

"I understand that you find in this affair the salt of your past passions; I beg you dear friend; do not get too close to this kind of hysteria."

(*) The Star LONDON. TUESDAY, 11 SEPTEMBER, 1888

The family of this unfortunate Annie Chapman has organized a secret funeral so as not to avoid being bothered by a crowd of onlookers. Even Warren complains about newspaper pressure, which is not to displease me. Men in herds are no better than stupid beasts!

"Who is ready to follow any shepherd says Melville!"

"Yes, everybody has his own theory. Like Lord Osborne and his "Jill the Ripper" ... A jealous woman ... its nonsense. I believe more in the guilt of Issenschmidt or Charles Ludwig who was arrested not so long ago. The idiot who gave himself up the other day, John Fitzgerald, was just an outcast full of nonsense."

"It's annoying," said Melville disdainfully, "It seems that I am grasping at straws."

"Maybe not so much. Yesterday, September 27, the Central News Agency received a letter dated on the 25th, which was brought to us. Dear Boss; this letter that would have been written by the killer."

"Interesting! What is it saying?"

"I do not know if I should tell you about it. I would not like us to find ourselves inundated by the mail of all the wacky Londoners..."

"Oh! As soon as the news is made public, all the nosy parkers of the press will jump on it."

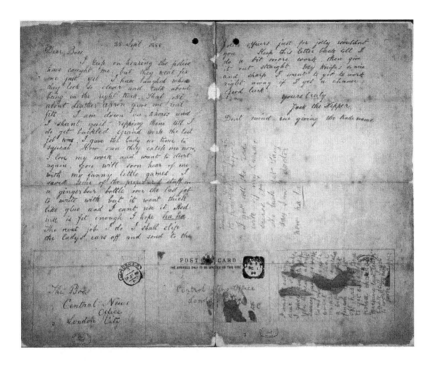

"Very good. You must swear that you will not talk to your friend the journalist Sims!"

Melville raised two fingers in the air.

"I swear!"

I pulled a document written in red ink from a file. It was a two-page letter to Charles Warren. The author called him "Dear boss", he indicated that he would cut the ears of his next victim and it was signed "Jack the Ripper".

My friend remained silent. He was deep in thought, his fiery eyes piercing me.

"Jack ... The Ripper ... It sounds so vulgar! One would think that of a vulgar field rendered!

Nemo is a much more distinguished name. He was breathing through his nose like an irritated thoroughbred, and went on; it's probably just a hoax!"

"Sure... It will not improve this mess. Scotland yard is playing its reputation."

"All I wish is for this imbroglio to cause Warren's downfall. This pest has been here for too long!"

"You would be a great successor!"

Melville seemed more relaxed. He raised his glass of beer.

"I propose a toast to Nemo, the instrument of his loss!"

His laughter echoed on the velvet upholstered walls.

9

Saturday, September 29, 1888
Berner Street; Whitechapel

Matthew Packer draws in his stall, and serves the big man with broad shoulders. He had already seen this great person several times. Like all his other clients, he was just one silhouette among many. For Matthew the hand that gives the money is more important than the face. He notices the furrows, the width of the palm, the shape and thickness of the individual's fingers; he retains only the middle and often the smell. All this was quickly forgotten in his daily routine.

Matthew Packer / Frédérick Abberline

A client with a dark moustache? Maybe he was blond? Most men with a moustache who came into his shop. Packer gave the half-pound of black grapes to the man; who spoke in a hoarse voice. The Bricklayer's Arms. The broad-brimmed sailor cap he wore lowered politely with a restrained force. He put his purchase in a coat pocket and headed for *Settle Street*. **This man was Jack.**

The Bricklayer's Arms was located at the corner of brown and packed buildings; it was a meeting point for all the night owls in the district. Elizabeth Stride called Long Liz; was doing the sidewalk. She had just left her man and she was playing with the white and red flower she wore on the back of her long black shredded woollen jacket.

"Black grapes!" Say Jack, addressing her.

He took a nice bunch of black grapes out of his pocket. She saw the juicy grains and under her little crepe hat she smiled. They chatted briefly, and set off together on Commercial Road, as a harmless couple. They crossed the road to the buildings of the school board. In *Berner Street* they walked along the Jewish Socialist Club. A melancholy, but energetic Slavic music escaped from the windows.

Male voices sang psalms from the Middle Ages, incomprehensible to passers by, from the top.

The festive atmosphere became less audible in front of the entrance to Dutfield Yard, a secluded and depressing spot. Long Liz entered, followed by Jack, to walk a few meters in a dark passage, just for some intercourse with a client, and was a sufficient distance for Elizabeth.

No way to go further in this disgusting place. This corner scared her. Jack urged her to go further and further into the unknown. At first she thought he was a nuisance. She pushed him away. When she felt the pressure from behind on her body, she realized she wasn't just in the presence of some ugly man. The man was determined to prevent her from getting out of this disgusting hole. She began to panic, to move, to hit the chest that was blocking her exit. It was in vain! Jack turned her over and slammed her against the wall with the strength of a bull.

Faithful pushed his knee into Liz's back and pulled the red scarf with all his strength. She uttered three faint, muffled cries, she was being asphyxiated. She slid gently to the ground. Long Liz hardly made any movement; she could see the shining curved blade that came closer to her neck, a real sorcerer's dagger. Without hesitation, he planted the weapon in the woman's throat. The blood gushed out of her trachea in small spurts.

Elizabeth's body was sprawled. It was almost nothing but flesh.

Israel Schwartz watched this scene from a distance, uncomprehending, indecisive and paralyzed. What are these two silhouettes doing? Is this a man who assaults a woman? What does he do to her? Looks like he ... He scratched his beard nervously.

Within a few seconds Jack had completed his bloody task. He quickly wiped the blade of the dagger and his hands on Liz's clothes. He glanced at his surroundings. The curved knife returned to its leather case, which he hid in his cloak. He saw Israel standing motionless in the near direction, a man was crossing the street, and behind him a big man was also coming out of the club. The later approached slowly trying to light his pipe with insistence... Coming from another street, Jack heard the rumble of a cart approaching. The bell of Christ Church sounded one o'clock in the morning.

He got up and shouted "Lipsky! (*). He attracted the attention of both men. His cry petrified them enough for Jack to run in the direction of Israel Schwartz, who became frightened and fled too.

*Antisemitic insult since Israel Lipsky's hanging for poisoning.

The cart came swinging on the pavement. The killer was already far away. The driver Diemschultz stopped in front of Long Liz's body. He leaned over; she was dead.

Jack hurried away and made a brief assessment of his situation. He knew that the Police were already converging on the crime scene. He went around Cable Street and arrived at Duke Street, he was out of danger, but his thirst for blood was not quenched. He adjusted his sailor's cap to a visor sheet of the same dark fabric. He tied a red scarf around his neck. He passed PC Harvey, who greeted him.

One hundred yards further; Catherine Eddowes walked on the heel of her patched boots. The rain had just stopped. She was a short, auburn haired woman, wearing a straw hat, adorned with false pearls, sewn in green and black velvet. She looked like a lady of the world. Looking closer, one could see it was only pretence. Everything was wrong: fur ruffles and buttons. Everything was just vulgar junk. He offered her six pence for intercourse. They walked together while talking. He was hardly paying attention to her beautiful hazel eyes. He did not need to estimate the age of his prey. She was a poor woman in her forties, weakened by a life of misery. Jack saw three men coming out of the Imperial Club on the other side of Duke Street.

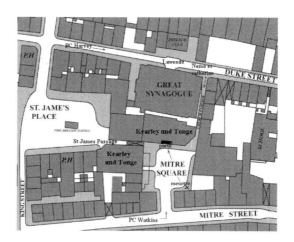

Jack and the prostitute were talking for a few moments at the crossing of Church Passage. The three men met the couple at around 1.34. He turned his head away; he had already seen one of the three men, the cigarette dealer; Joseph Lawende.

The couple entered Church Passage. In Mitre Square Catherine felt an uncontrollable shiver run down her spine. The place was bathed in darkness, shrouded in mist. A sinister atmosphere, evocative of a muddy cemetery, the air filled with decomposing gases. The lamppost emitted an unusually weak glow. She could scarcely see it; unable to suspect that he had come the day before, to sabotage the single gas-spout that lit up the square. He dragged her to the darkest corner of Mitre Square against a wooden door. In contrast to the square; the words written on the *Kearley &* *Tonge* facade spread out unseen on the walls invaded by darkness.

She walked with an indecisive step followed by Jack, holding his twisted red scarf tightly in his left hand. He slipped the scarf around Catherine's neck, choking her in an instant. Like a bird caught in the claws of a feral cat; she struggled without hope. He laid her on the ground. The curved blade came out of the lapel of his coat.

In order to present her neck to the sacrifice, he pushed her head towards her shoulder. A thick red line was traced on the throat. It was the knife that killed Catherine Eddowes, blood spurting from the neck of the unfortunate woman.

The demented ambidextrous surgeon was planting the weapon under the defenceless sternum, shearing the tissues and flesh to the pubis. He breathed deeply, calmly, focused on the body. The disturbance of the lamp left him more time to act. The belly was cut in several places, allowing him, once again, to pull the viscous intestines, to draw bloody trimmings on Catherine, then to carefully extract the left kidney and the uterus. He deposited this precious food in his victim's apron which he had just spread on the ground for the occasion. He had not finished his crime, using the curved knife as an artist's brush. He mutilated the face of his victim, already grinning in death. Ears, cheeks and cheekbones were sliced almost as a game. Jack acted thus whilst feeling detached from the situation, like a spectator.

A kind of dissociated state between pleasure and curiosity. Catherine had become a terrifying shape.

At one forty-four in the morning he was done when he saw a PC light coming from Mitre Street.

Without hesitation he crossed the square and he quickly opened the door to *Kearley and Tonge* with his key. Jack slowly closed the door without slamming it. Jack knew that the night watchman was working in the accounting department in the other part of the building. He climbed the stairs to his office with his rubber soled shoes. He took off his bloodied clothes. He washed his hands; put the kidney in a jar filled with alcohol, and the uterus in another jar. He carefully put them in his closet with his disguise and closed the lock. When everything was in order; he went to the window and saw PC Watkins who was lighting Mitre Square with his big bull's-eye lamp.

Watkins / Eddowes / Mitre Square

He watched, amused, hidden on the second floor; the policeman progressed hesitantly to the body; raised his lantern with an outstretched arm. In the impenetrable darkness that reigned in Mitre Square, the gleam illuminated the battered cobblestones. Jack knew that the policeman was under the shock of the horrible vision. PC Edward Watkins mumbled a few words. He took his whistle, raised it to his trembling lips. A shrill sound pierced the surroundings alerting the neighbourhoods of the new atrocity. The policeman looked in every corner, still shaken by his discovery. He found Kearley and Tonge's door ajar, and gently pushed it. Worried, he made a call inside. The night watchman George Morris alerted by the commotion; came running holding a broom in his hand.

"For God's sake, friend, come to my help!" cried the PC gesticulating wildly.

"Wait! I am going to get my lamp; the gas lamp in the place hardly gives any light anymore!"

Watkins looked at his watch... an hour and forty-seven. Morris came back almost immediately.

"What is going on?"

"Oh my God! ... There is another woman ... Cut in pieces!"

Morris says.

"Where is she?"

"In the corner!"

They ran across the square. The blood of the two men froze. Were they living this nightmare together? The light of their lamps illuminated the mutilated, lifeless body, offered to the city as a horrible gift. Watkins whistled almost to the point of losing his breath. After ten minutes PC Harvey and PC Holland arrived from Duke Street. Watkins was eager to seek help. Still dazed, George Morris remained still like a stone statue, in the company of the policeman.

About two o'clock in the morning when Dr. Sequeira leaned over the late Catherine. She was still lying in the square. The doctor made a long observation, looking closely at all the wounds. Ten minutes later came a cart to take away the corpse. At twenty minutes past two, Mitre Square had emptied; the police had left to escort the body.

Jack had observed everything from his post, both anxious and excited.

He saw George Morris enter the building, closing the door, heading for the other part of the building. His usual resting place was no longer safe. The killer waited another ten minutes before swapping clothes. An idea had sprouted in his evil spirit.

Jack took a white chalk on the edge of his blackboard; slipped it into his pocket. He took the bloody half-apron, after wrapping it with another piece of clean cloth. Jack was thinking fast! Between Berner Street, and Mitre Square; which street was a good place to leave the torn apron with a little phrase that would set the Jewish district on fire?

He went out of the building secretly, passed by St Aldgate Street, then Whitechapel Road. He walked past a PC, but he was so discreet and anonymous that it had no consequence.

He turned left to Goulston Street. In this street halfway between the two crimes were houses full of immigrants.

It was at the entrance to No. 119 Whentworth that he pulled out the chalk from his pocket. He began to trace the inscription at two thirty five in the morning.

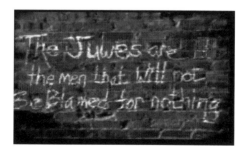

« The Juwes are the men that will not be blamed for nothing »

Jack was certain that the word "Juwes" would not leave the friends of William Morris indifferent, the men who were reciting medieval poems in that socialist club at 40 Berner Street. Impassive, he placed the apron, tainted with Catherine Eddowe's blood, on the ground. Her fleshy body was now being tossed like a sack of potatoes by the cart that took her to the morgue.

The connection between the two murders would be made easily. The Jews had prevented him from completing his work on Berner Street, it was their fault. He had to commit a second murder to remove the kidney and the uterus, a symbol of procreation for him. His salvation depended on their absorption. The ritual was immoral but imperative.

Only one true brave, authentic warrior can transcend all limits. Jack was so excited by his future meal that he swore to tell the rest of the world. A small anonymous letter with half the kidney of his last victim would do the trick. His pocket watch indicated two forty-five.

He headed north, with a quiet step. As usual he took the train to reach his home, with the satisfaction of having accomplished his mission. His mind was already anticipating the tumult that would seize London.

James Monro hunts the ghost of Jack the Ripper

The Star will break all sales records, and articles against police chief Charles Warren will feed the many newspapers in the capital. (*)

* Daily News United Kingdom 1 October 1888
Two dreadful murders were committed yesterday morning in or near the East-end
* Evening News London, U.K. 1 October 1888
THE REIGN OF TERROR IN WHITECHAPEL.AT THE SCENE OF THE CRIMES ON SUNDAY
* Morning Advertiser (London) 1 October 1888
The bodies of two women, both with their throats cut, and one of them abdominally mutilated
* Pall Mall Gazette 1 October 1888
MORE HORRORS IN THE EAST END TWO WOMEN MURDERED THE SAME FEARFUL MUTILATION
* The Star LONDON. MONDAY, 1 OCTOBER, 1888.
THE terror of Whitechapel has walked
* Times (London) Monday, 1 October 1888

Two more murders must now be added to the black list of similar crimes of which the East-end of London has very lately been the scene.

96

10
Saturday, October 13
9 Tite Street; Westminster; London

"Mr & Mrs James Monro."

9 Tite Street

The butler slipped away to let us in; my wife Ruth and I. Behind the bourgeois facade of 9 *Tite Street*; the salon offered the spectacle of the entire Macnaghten family.

A charming little English family, children playing quietly; a woman seated pensive in a leather sofa and a father in his chair by the fireside.

Dora Emily Macnaghten was a lovely person; a delicate brunette woman with fine features. She wore black lace around her neck adorned with a small mother-of-pearl flower. Her clothes showed the financial comfort of her husband. Melville stopped his task and came to greet us. Obeying a command from their mother's hand, the children stopped playing, and ran towards the guests.

Julia Mary had just celebrated her seventh birthday and Charles was about 9 years old. They had that serious look of well-behaved children. They watched us; intrigued by our faces they had seen a few years earlier, on another continent without being able to recognize us. Their faces displayed both of their parents' features. Charles had the same eyes as his mother in the middle of his little round head, and Julia Mary her father's firm body, which one guessed fit for the races in the parks and the climbing of trees. They were dressed like all the Englishmen of good family, starched collar, short trousers for the boy and a long tartan skirt for the girl.

"Ruth! What a pleasure to see you at last! James, come in!"

Dora got up, handed me a delicate hand that I seized with deference. Her kind smile and beautiful eyes gave her an aura of tenderness to soften the heart of the most cynical.

"You are as beautiful as in my memory Madam!"

"Oh! Please, James, call me Dora, we are no longer strangers."

She laughed quietly, took my hand, and took a step back.

Melville bowed to my wife.

"My dear Ruth!"

He took her hand, and bent softly.

"My very dear friend."

My wife fluttered her eyelashes. It was hard to resist Melville's charisma. There was something of an animal in his manner, like a tiger who deigns to show affection, a wild beast purring. She giggled, under his magnetic spell. He straightened up and came to greet me. The two women greeted each other as long-time old friends. They had not seen each other since India, a perfect pretext for chatting.

"My friend!"

He gripped me by the shoulder with a master's grip, and slipped his other hand into mine. Since his return, he had always displayed his strong comradeship for me.

I could not help but think of the secret he confided to me about his relationship problems, when I saw this little picture of a perfect British household, the picture was completely skewed.

«You have come in spite of this detestable weather, I applaud your courage! What's more, with a frightful cannibal lurking in London!"

"Cannibal?"

"Yes, you know, this horrible monster!"

Melville, without moving, pointed to his children. I realized that he did not wish to pronounce the word killer or assassin in their presence, and that the word cannibal was used to give a whimsical impression, like a character in an adventure novel. Dora gave me a tight smile.

"Oh! Do not worry; I have my rifle with me, as in India!"

The children's eyes lit up; I made a mistake; speaking of a rifle. They could not hold up anymore and wondered where the rifle was.

"Uh!" Later… Mr Monro has just arrived" said Dora. "

"He certainly doesn't want to go back in the rain to show you. Aren't your father's rifles enough for you?"

There was almost contempt in this last sentence. Melville showed no signs of trouble.

"Please, do not stay that way, take a good chair."

"Reginald, please tell Miss Mellor to look after the children, and remind her that they will be eating with us at seven o'clock."

Melville showed me a splendid leather chair.

"A glass of Brandy?"

"With pleasure!"

My friend made a sign to another servant who had remained in a corner of the room. He was dressed like an English valet, with the coppery skin of a Raj native.

"Did you bring him back in your suitcases?" I say jokingly about the valet.

"He did not want to leave us when we left. A real drama! He was crying like a child being torn from his mother. We kept him. He is an excellent handyman, coupled with an outstanding tracker. I often took him for our hunts, do you remember?"

"Not really. They are all the same to my eyes."

Melville laughs complacently.

"He is a wonderful guardian for children; he is ferocious as a wolf, and faithful as a dog."

"I admit that he has a beautiful build."

"You're not mistaken; he is an old Gurkha."

The servant displayed a mask of impassibility which commanded respect. His dark eyes left no doubt about his ability to kill.

"Ghurkhas are war machines as comfortable with a cutlass as a rifle. One would not dream of a better bodyguard."

"Dear Melville, are not you afraid that your swarthy friend will worry the crowds? Rumour has it that the famous ... hum ... cannibal as you called it would be a funny character."

"I do not hide from you that he catches the eye! Do not worry, he is loyalty incarnate, and he never gets out of here; except to accompany the children to school."

Madame Macnaghten seemed absent. Her eyes were blank; it was clear that she was not interested in the discussion at all.

"Well, my friend with your boy Charles you have two men to defend you."

Melville was laughing and Dora was smiling an amused smile. The imperturbable servant brought a tray; on which were placed four crystal glasses; and a bottle of Brandy. He served Ruth and Dora, myself, and Melville. He returned to his corner like the bird from a cuckoo clock. I continued to observe the decor.

I noticed several paintings representing the landscapes of Bombay and Calcutta. I pointed out with my glass a beautiful Leopard skin spread on the ground.

"Oh, that?" Said Melville. "A skin I brought back from Kishnaghur. Do you want me to tell you the whole story?"

"With pleasure!"

"Very well ... A week before the hunt for this leopard I was on horseback, a hot wind was blowing from the south; when suddenly my horse slipped and fell on top of me, injuring my leg. Confined to the house; I was bored when villagers came to warn me that leopard tracks had been found on the edge of the jungle about a mile from us. I was not able to walk, and a tonjon (a kind of open sedan chair) was put at my disposal, I decided to leave for the hunt. A crowd had already gathered at the scene and the hubbub it provoked inevitably displeased the Leopard, who was starting to move away. We started on his trail, when at last I saw the wild beast above the tall grass. Sitting in my room, I fired immediately and hit him, without killing him. A nice mess! The leopard was now hurt; it was like having the devil near the village." (*)

(*) Days of my Years - Melville Macnaghten 1914 p 44 à 52.

"I was hobbling around the Barbary cane field, where he seemed to have taken refuge, when the village postman who was with me suddenly stopped in front of me, pointing at the jungle, saying, Look Sahib, he is there ! I had often heard that a wounded leopard turned to attack the hunter. I can testify that this is true. In an instant, like a ball of fire, he had jumped on the native, and had hastily retreated towards the grove. I had straightened the man, who was as brave as possible.

He had been bitten on the right shoulder, and severely scratched at the bottom of his chest. The cat's bite was as harmful as his claws. The animal's bacteria are as fatal to the wounded man as poisonous arrows ... I took him home to have his wounds quickly disinfected. The beast was still prowling. On the way to our hunt, we came across a coolie who was hunting 'ortolan' for his master. He only had an old shotgun. We explained to him what was going on, and I asked him to load a bullet into his gun. Which he did immediately, then he plunged into the jungle, belly down. For a quarter of an hour, there was a heavy silence, when suddenly ... bang!

A shot rang out, frightening the birds. My coolie came out of the undergrowth: dragging the remains of a huge leopard.

He told me that the beast had crawled like a snake until he found himself facing him. When he pulled the trigger; the barrel of the musket touched the skin of the beast!

Above the leopard's spotted shoulder, there was indeed a small hole; perfectly clear."

Fascinated by his story I exclaimed:

"You will not prevent me from thinking you are a first class tracker and hunter!

You hit him first, and without the hindrance of your leg wound, you would have killed him yourself. I think you would have no trouble tracking criminals in the streets of London."

"Your flattery touches me, James, if I'm not mistaken; there is already this gentleman Lusk and his mob that patrol Whitechapel night and day in Whitechapel to stop the murderer."

Dora took advantage of this topic to start the conversation.

"Yes! James, what about this madman? I read the newspapers, London lives in fear. Yet, I am a woman who has lived in India for many years. I witnessed many revolts, violence. But right now, a monster lurks in my dear city. Forgive my vehemence, but I cannot believe that the English soil can engender such degeneration in a human soul."

"You think a Briton can not be able to do that?"

"Absolutely! I have one more argument: never can an Englishman go after poor women. Oh, I do not live in fairy tales; far from it; I know that a man sometimes, can kill a woman. But to have killed how many already? Four in a row! I know they are women of little virtue, and those men sometimes, feel the need to trade with them."

Dora was silent for a few moments, and looked at us insistently, especially at her husband.

Ruth nodded at her friend's speech with a grave and silent air.

Melville's wife went on.

"And to disembowel them? A Brit, I repeat, seems unable to do that!"

"Dora your explanation seems a little rigid; answered Melville, ask James, he is a daily witness to the turpitudes and depths of the human soul... don't you agree, James?"

"Yes, absolutely my dear, I can assure you that I have witnessed things that propriety forbids me to name here. As proof of this terrible affair, there are details that would make you lose sleep for months Dora."

"You'll tell me that in my office later, after dinner" Melville said wryly. I love these bloody details that scare women!

Dora gave me a furious look. We were conversing until dinner time, focusing on the current crimes that fascinated the United Kingdom. The heavy ticking of the clock punctuated our conversation. Ruth and Dora lamented the lack of information about these murders, which I said was for the best. Detective Abberline and his associates did not need the curiosity of the crowds. The conversation turned to the rewards offered for the capture of this madman.

At the beginning of October, a notable Londoner, Lord Mayor had agreed to give five hundred pounds for all information leading to the capture of the Whitechapel murderer, the decision was almost immediately revoked by the Minister Henri Mattews. Dora and Ruth claimed that such methods could catch the culprit more quickly, since the whole community of Londoners would participate in the hunt!

I opposed it, defending the police, with a jaded bitterness; my arguments at the moment did not weigh heavily considering the lack of results. Our two wives stuck firmly to their position. Indignation was the feeling they shared with most Star readers.

The silence of the police and the apathy of the minister disappointed them. Melville said nothing, just watching the debate with amusement. He gently winked at me, saying; "Let our lovely wives talk." Reginald entered the room and announced; the meal is served. Melville stood up, unfolding his tall stature, and invited me cordially to pass into the dining room. The two companions followed us. The dining room was decorated in the same style as the living room, luxurious, weighed down with thick red velvet curtains. In the middle of the room stood a sturdy wooden table, around which were placed six seats.

With great coordination, the children arrived at the same time as us, through another door, and sat quietly in their places.

"Oh! My friends, we did not ask you for news of your children. How are Charles and Douglas doing?" Dora asked in the sorry tone of someone who lacks the basic rules of courtesy.

"Like charms," I replied, sitting down. They are already great fellows Charles, the eldest is twenty-five years old and the youngest in the family; Douglas fourteen years old.

At the table, the dish was brought solemnly, covered with a bell that the servant removed to serve a beef curry.

Wine was entitled to the same protocol. Reginald presented it to his master, who nodded in silence, then served the guests.

"Coming back to our previous conversation, we were talking about this odious Warren."

Little Charles came out of his silence; he had information that allowed him to talk with grown-ups.

"Warren? It's the mean man, he says with the pride of a schoolboy who knows his lesson by heart."

"Charles, please be quiet," said Dora firmly, "we do not talk at dinner when there are adults.

The boy obeyed. Ruth tenderly placed her hand over his chest.

"Oh! Poor little angel, he wants to show us his knowledge!

Melville affectionately ruffled the hair of the blonde head, who looked surprised by this unusual gesture."

"This little guy has fine ears. I'm like you, James, I do not like him."

"He's incompetent; I'm not teaching you anything. His methods are obsolete, he does not believe in the usefulness of the inspectors! On the contrary, they are the ones we need most; smart men, able to follow a track and investigate rationally."

"It is necessary to fence the crime scenes, so that onlookers do not destroy evidence the indices. We must rely on the flair of police dogs; organize organise manhunts with detective agencies. Obvious things ... except for Warren. What matters to him are his grotesque outfits and the shoe polish of his men! I suppose you read the statistics that the Star newspaper had published the day before yesterday. The observation is simple: we are dramatically short of men. How do you want to work effectively without sufficient staff? Does Warren do anything to stop this? No. He does not move a finger. The boat is sinking and he still believes he can navigate. I only regret one thing: because of his incompetence, there will surely be new victims."

Ruth put her hand on my forearm.

"James, please, there are children at the table."

"Oh! Excuse me, I got carried away."

"It's nothing James" said Melville. "If the cannibal (he was talking to his boy and his daughter) was still eating someone, it certainly will not be grandchildren! That's it, let's not talk about it, Melville concludes coldly. We'll be in my office later, James, if you do not mind."

"Of course, of course, with pleasure, my friend."

The rest of the dinner was most enjoyable. Reginald brought us the dessert, a superb pudding. Melville leaned over and whispered in my ear:

"Maybe this is the right time to go to my office? How about a good cigar? We could resume this exciting discussion of earlier. You have not been able to say everything, and I have questions for you!"

After a few moments I noticed that Dora and Ruth were heading for the living room. A nurse took the children away.

"I gave a quick wave to my wife, who told her I was leaving her a few minutes. She turned her head and nodded with a small smile."

"Good, James, if you please accompany me."

Melville led the way and I followed him to his office. In the room; buffalo horns adorned the walls; and on a low table sat a stuffed jackal, fangs protruding into an open mouth. There was an atmosphere of oppression in the room, exacerbated by the multitude of weapons on display.

I noted between rifles swords and pistols; the characteristic shape of a kukri.

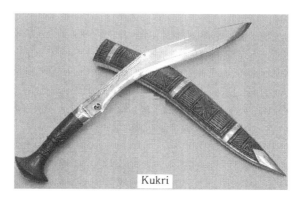

Kukri

"I knew you're a good hunter, Melville, but not that good. You killed them all?"

"Yes. I could not expose all my hunting trophies. My record is seven jackals killed in the same day."

"That's a lot!" He said, amused by my absorbed air.

Melville pulled out a wooden box, adorned with Indian motives. It contained beautiful cigars, he offered me one, and the smell of fresh tobacco tickled my nostrils.

"Please James, make yourself comfortable!"

He invited me to sit in a sublime leather studded chair.

"A glass of cognac?"

He also took out a crystal carafe and two glasses. I accepted his offer. Seen from the armchair, the office seemed less imposing, more muffled. The smell of cigar and alcohol relaxed me. Melville sat at his desk, like a king in his castle, grabbed a cigar, offered me a light, and lit his own.

A light haze gradually invaded the room, diffusing a delicate smell of dry grass and cinnamon.

"Well" he said, "Let's stay with Charles Warren. Do you really think he can continue?"

"Warren does not have control of the situation. I'm going to make a prediction: I'm almost certain he's going to resign. It has been a long time since the unease started, since the beginning of July in truth. It must be said that the Bloody Sunday of last year made him unpopular with the people. With each new murder comes a new outcry. Look at the Star: every day there is an article against him. It's awful, I'm almost hoping for a new crime, so he can not do anything but resign!"

"You do not think what you're saying, my friend, its anger that makes you talk," Melville told me affably.

Let's stop talking about it. This man is doomed, that's all.

"Excuse my anger; I can not stand his incompetence, especially in these circumstances.

113

We must stop the Ripper!"

My friend was frowning.

"You too call him the Ripper? I hate that name."

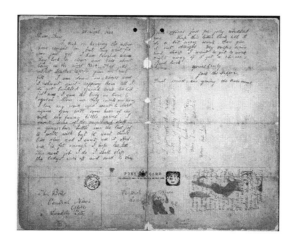

"Me too, but this nickname is on everyone's lips, since the letter, Dear Boss signed Jack the Ripper of the twenty-fifth of September, and a few days later, the postcard Saucy Jack of October 1st reinforced the idea." (*)

"The press has encouraged the use of this nickname. We ourselves had the weakness to authorise the publication of facsimiles of these letters to try to confuse the author."

"Yes! I saw them ... hoaxes probably the work of a journalist. My friend G. Sims told me that Frederic Best, a man working for the paper, would have written with his friend, Thomas John Bulling, at the request of his superior from the Central News Agency, Charles Moore."

"That's why I want you to enter the Yard: You understand that too. These letters only serve to increase the circulation of the Star and other newspapers." Melville drew pensively on his cigar.

"Maybe the real Nemo will eventually send a letter! It will be lost in the mass of false letters!"

"Probably!"

My host seemed lost in thought.

"Jack the Ripper ... Dear Boss ... Completely silly!" Melville mumbled the name the press had unveiled. I watched the clouds of smoke rise on the ceiling.

Melville's voice broke the silence:

"It was dark ... With my horse I followed a band of jackals. Suddenly, I heard the barking of my dogs. I galloped in their direction to a rocky promontory. That's when I saw her. An imposing female jackal separated from her companions and cornered by my dogs. It was a beautiful beast, graceful and majestic. With its white gaiters, it looked like a coquette, I assure you."

115

"I do not know what took me; I felt it was for me.

I jumped from my horse; took out my kukri and stealthily approached her. A kind of fever had gripped me; I felt like an animal ready to pounce. Something in me told me that I had to defeat her with my hands like a primitive man. Powder and balls are cheats; a good way for the weak ... The beast was too busy with my dogs to notice me. I had the impression that she was offered to me, that she was waiting for her fate. In my head, it was a hurricane of sensations.

When I was right behind her, a feeling of great power came over me: I had a life in the palm of my hand, free to take it or not...

I sliced her. She bled heavily, without a sound. I had immediately disembowelled her to give to the dogs; the spleen, the heart, and the loins. We had returned with this trophy." With his cigar he pointed at the magnificent remains of stuffed jackals that surrounded the table.

Melville was proud of this catch, and did not hide it. He told me that he had to kill a minimum of sixty jackals in India.

"Awesome."

"Isn' it?"

Once we had consumed our cigars, Melville had a look at his pocket watch.

"Heaven, our women must wait for us ... In the living room, Ruth and Dora were still chatting. At our sight, they offered us two kind faces. Dora's Dora was reminiscent of a blooming flower, despite her sad eyes formed the pistil. Ruth, older, still held the charm of her twenty years in my heart."

"It's getting late, I'm sorry to tell you that we are going to take leave, I have to get up early tomorrow, and the week will be particularly busy."

"Very good!" Said Melville

The servants brought us our coats. On the doorstep, Melville whispered in my ear.

"Do not worry, James, you're right Warren's days are numbered."

James Monro hunts the ghost of Jack the Ripper

11
Thursday, October 18, 1888
George Lusk; 1 Alderney Road

"A package for you Mr. Lusk."

Postman handed him the parcel. On the doorstep of his house he took the package with a puzzled look. It was a small piece of cardboard. On the top a nervous hand had scribbled the address: Mr George Lusk, 1 Alderney road, Mile End.

"Thank you. "

Strange! Moving the parcel close to his ear, he shook it. The weight of an object bumping across the edges could be heard. Odd ... George put the box down on the living room table.

"Who is it?" He asks his wife.

"I do not have the faintest idea..."

"What are you waiting for, open it!"

George was running. He took the knife out of his pocket and cut the string. With his fingertips he opened the package.

"What is it? He mumbled."

And inside were a letter and a small piece of flesh. Between his thumb and forefinger, he examined the piece of meat.

"It's meat."

He dropped it on the table in the direction of his wife. The sheet sponged the brown liquid was oozing from it, drenching the sheet in a red halo. The letter disturbed him even more. It was addressed to him personally with an uneducated handwriting full of spelling mistakes:

"From Hell

Mr Lusk,

Sir,

I send you a half kidney, which I took from a woman, kept for you, the other end I fried and ate it was very good, I can send you the knife that ripped it only if you wait a little longer

Signed: catch me when you can, Mister Lusk»

George raised an eyebrow. There was something sick in this message, he had seen too much, both as leader of the Vigilante Committee and all his life. Another hoax, he thought.

It's weird! Said his wife

The package ended the day in one of his secretary's drawers...

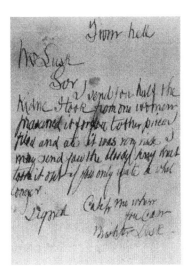

The next day, George Lusk carried his strange item to the Vigilance Committee meeting. The hoax made a sensational impression. A sort of tumult vibrated in the assembly. Warren's name was spoken several times. The chief commissioner was the main culprit: if he had done his job, and stopped the Ripper, there would be no such horrors today. Lusk, certain he was dealing with a morbid joke, did not insist. But the famous piece of kidney, cut in half, was so much in the minds of some of the committee members that Aarons, Harris, Reeves and Lawton decided to visit Lusk a few hours later. In spite of their anxiety and obstinacy, the president replied that he had nothing to do with it. He would throw away the package, the letter and half of the kidney.

It took a lot of patience and explanation to persuade him to bring this macabre package to an expert in anatomy. Dr Wiles, a neighbouring surgeon, the perfect opportunity to find out if this organ was really that of the murdered woman Dr. Frederick Wiles was not there; his assistant had the idea of taking him to another practitioner; Dr. Thomas Openshaw who worked at the London Hospital, just a stone's throw away. It was only after this journey that a man of science bent over the case, and concluded: "We are in the presence of a left half-kidney ... Human! That of a person suffering from nephritis". The joke became more and more morbid. They could not keep it a secret. The next day, the letter and the piece of kidney were given to the police. (*)

(*) Evening News London, U.K. 19 October 1888FIFTH EDITION. HALF THE VICTIM'S MISSING KIDNEY RESTORED. THE OTHER HALF EATEN BY THE CANNIBAL ASSASSIN

12
Thursday, November 8, 1888
Sir Charles Warren resigns

"... and because of that, to accept my resignation".

Warren added a few lines of courtesy, nervously signed the letter. He took the sheet, read it calmly, folded the letter carefully, and put it in a blank envelope. He looked at the constable, who was waiting, watching him attentively. He handed the letter with a dry gesture. The police officer seized it, bowed respectfully, and went out. For a few moments, the commissioner remained seated, his back straight, a posture imposed by his military style jacket, with a stiff cut.

"No more of this", he fell softly against the back of his chair, shattered. He sighed. It is done!

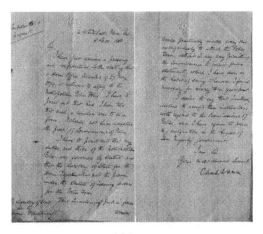

There was still a copy of Murray's Magazine on the desk. His main article, the Police of the Metropolis, eighteen long pages, all about the London Police Force, had been the straw that broke the camel's back. Minister Matthews did not appreciate his giving his opinion without permission in the police diary. On November 6th, he was sanctioned. In Warren's head, the desire to leave the Scotland Yard had already been dwelling for a long time. From the beginning, he had been criticized from the beginning, he had resisted ... He had not won. The people and the Home office had got the better of him. The man in the street, who barely knew his face, despised him, since the horrible events of November 13, 1887 in Trafalgar Square, called Bloody Sunday.

The radical newspapers, Pall Mall Gazette and the Star in the lead, after denigrating the police for the riots of 1886 and 1887, had turned their attention to the Whitechapel Horrors.

After the murders of Emma Smith, then Martha Tabram, the sales took off, and the publications rivalled each other with more and more sordid articles, sparing no detail, adding insult to injury by publishing false letters like the infamous Dear Boss of September 25th. All these horrors, all this insanity were all about one person: Charles Warren. He was accused of interference, of laziness.

He was accused of not understanding, of not doing the right thing when necessary. Not to put enough men on the ground. When he listened to a remark saying that the police were missing too many bloodhounds, he sent for two dogs; Barnaby and Bhurgho. Immediately, the newspaper criticised him for being obsessed with them. Jack the Ripper would always run...

For a brief moment, he wondered what could happen if he stayed? Would he end up catching the killer?

In analyzing the situation, he realized that he lived at untouchable heights for the killer. The victims were nothing but girls. He had already threatened to resign at the same time as Monro. Matthews had only accepted his opponent's resignation. And again the minister had promoted Monro; he had promoted him to "Head of the Special Branch of Intelligence " a position he himself coveted!

He felt ignored, pushed aside. Even Queen Victoria sent a telegram to Minister Robert Arthur Talbot:

"I call for more effective action by the police forces.

There was another terrible murder.

I demand police reinforcements, I want more detectives in the streets, and we need to put in place better public lighting.

I wonder if the crimes of Ripper would not be committed by a sailor of passage. Please indicate this item for verification to the police forces.

Signed Victoria, September 3, 1888 »

Matthews had not been able to support him and everything was blamed on him. There were so many meshes that it was impossible to disentangle them. At least we could point this article from Murray's magazine, The Police of the Metropolis. The ultimate incident!

Warren took a look at his agenda: it was November 8, 1888, his last day as commissioner.

13
Friday, November 9, 1888
Dorset Street

The Ten Bells pub had been a gathering place for centuries for the residents of Whitechapel. On its front window was painted the date of its creation in 1666. The year of the great fire of London. The number of bells inscribed corresponded to the number of bells installed in the neighbouring church.

THE TEN BELLS since 1666

In the evening, the Ten Bells were filled with various souls: harassed workers, apprentices, craftsmen, little hands, prostitutes. The inhabitants of the beautiful quarters said that in this pub of Whitechapel, the dregs of humanity gathered.

In truth, there were only men and women seeking entertainment after twelve, or fourteen hours of hard work, the prejudices of the upper class were not quite false, criminals, thieves and prostitutes could also be found in this pub. The high society had created those individuals for whom the only way to show their disobedience, was to lose themselves in an alcoholic haze and a prostitute's bosom. This ephemeral rebellion was reflected, inside the Ten Bells, by the strident sounds of the violin which punctuated furious dances, the shrieks and the clinking of the clashing glasses. From outside, the pub shone with a thousand lights: by the light of the lights were reflected in the mirrors and the zinc. Inside, thick tobacco smoke gripped the customer's throat, a strong smell of beer making its way into the back of the nostrils. Hands clung to the sticky walls of frying vapours; eyes were dazzled by the sight of the numerous crowd.

Jack was enjoying a pint of ginger beer when he heard a drunken woman at the next table talking about her misfortunes...

"I lived with a worker, when he lost his job, I had to earn the bread from home and so I came down ... It's a life of suffering.

If you knew how many times I almost lost my life.

James Monro hunts the ghost of Jack the Ripper

One day I left with a client, a sailor. We went to a discreet alleyway to do our business and would you believe it, he tried to strangle me! Luckily our good Lord up there was watching huh? Because just then a cop came up from behind a cab and drove this bastard away. He was a detective and a gentleman, for sure, one who had rubber soles. Finally ... it's my lot. Since that day, every night after supper, I'm taking to the streets hoping to meet the sailor. I hope that this time, he will finish the job!" (*)

Jack was looking at his pocket watch ... one-thirty in the morning; the time of his appointment was approaching. That night, there were a lot of people. He left his noisy hiding place, which he had kept a secret for thirty five years. On top of his freshly dyed black hair, he put on his soft felt hat; he put down his soft felt. The shadow of the hat hid his piercing gaze. He pulled up the collar of his long black coat, trimmed at the collar and wrists with astrakhan fur, masking his broad shoulders and tall stature.

Someone less attentive to the general hustle and bustle would have noticed the details of his costume: dark gaiters, boots with gold buttons, gold chain connected to his pocket watch, black tie attached by a horseshoe pin.

(*) Days of my Years - Melville Macnaghten 1914 p 56-57

The white collar covering his neck gave him a hieratic air. With the hand that held his gloves, he pulled on the edge of he adjusted his moustache. His other hand was holding a bundle of clothes ... His stock a step that revealed his natural strength. Commercial Street was soaked, and the road worn by the cart wheels of the day and the rain had made the road muddy. Going down the street, he headed for to Britannia Pub. Under the lamp of No. 74 Pub Queen's Heard; he saw a tall, auburn haired, plump girl dressed in a Linsey dress adorned with a small white apron, with a red shawl pulled around her shoulders, she was chatting with a man. Jack crossed to the other side of the street without saying anything.

"George would give me six pence?"

"Impossible! I have nothing left; I've spent everything at the Romford pub!"

"Oh please, my dear new friend!"

"No Ginger! I have nothing for you!"

She tried to beg for a little longer, George Hutchinson, remained intractable. She could tell him that she needed those few coins, but her friend did not want to know anything. Mary Jane Kelly would not extort anything. It was ten past two when she abandoned him. She looked desperate, even her looks could not help her.

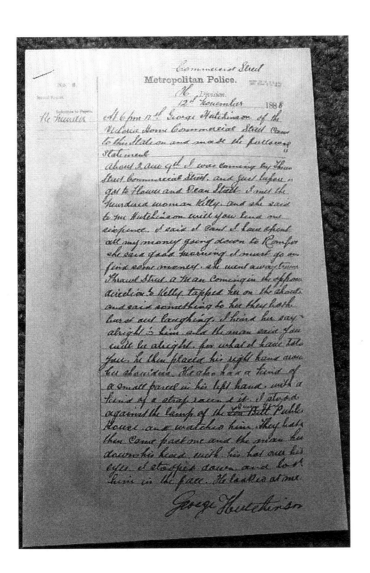

A sense of deep discouragement filled the prostitute, when she noticed the man who had met them a few minutes earlier; the man with the black coat. He had gravitated around them during their discussion, and now he was standing there. He walked towards Mary, and with a kind smile, he politely approached her.

"I have the money ... with a present."

Both burst out laughing ... such a distinguished customer, it felt like a gift from heaven and the assurance of earning far more than sixpence.

"Very good..."

"I have what you want, and in addition ... a small gift."

The man was laughing again, but almost childishly this time. In his left hand, there was a small bundle, tied by a strap. She did not pay attention to this item. If the man stammered a little, he was handsome and he was young, she thought. She replied with a smile. Despite her misery, she was lovely.

She felt even more beautiful when he put his right hand on her shoulder. A heavy reassuring hand that took her away from her torment. For a long time she had felt like a courtesan.

In her mind, she fancied herself a Parisian lady of the night, on the arm of an elegant young man, walking on the grand boulevards of the City of Light. Jack and Mary were walking to the Britannia on the corner of Dorset Street, George Hutchinson, who was still nearby, began to follow them.

They gave the innocuous impression of being just a pair of lovers when they stopped in front of the porch of a round entrance. The narrow passage led to a dark, gloomy and uninviting place, above a pediment. On the stone wall one could distinguish its name: Miller's Court.

Mary Jane's friend had followed the couple, seen and heard the whole discussion. No need to be a clairvoyant to guess the nature of the services the man asked of the woman. With a nod, she accepted.

"It's good, my dear. Come. You will be comfortable."

He put an arm around her shoulders, and he kissed her on the neck.

"I lost my handkerchief!"

The sentence was almost a test to see what kind of man she was dealing with. Without a word, he handed her a red handkerchief. He was a gentleman. She dragged him under the arch encircled with red bricks. George saw them disappear in the darkness.

They arrived in a tiny, elongated courtyard, lit by the faint light coming from a low window on the ground floor.

Thirteen was the number indicated above the door through which they entered. It was two thirty-five in the morning. George Hutchinson kept spying until three o'clock and then went home. The rain had begun to turn to a faint drizzle. At the same time, Mrs. Cox, a resident of 5-6 Miller's Court, entered her home. No sound, no light in Kelly's room. Madame Cox, exhausted, returned to her room, and soon fell into a deep sleep.

Mary was busy. She had carefully folded her clothes on a chair, while Jack undressed. In the dim light, he was lying on the bed, waiting naked.

The young body of Mary Jane Kelly was pleasant and curvaceous. Her twenty five years had not yet made her lose her freshness. Mary lit a candle, and the shadows highlighted her voluptuous curves and her firm breasts. She was slowly approaching the bed. Jack, lying down, stared at her strangely, examining her from head to toe. For a moment, she thought she could detect a glimmer of hope in her lover's eager eyes, a glimmer of hope mixed with anguish. This impression contrasted with the strength of his muscles and softened her heart, softened the young woman with light red hair. Sitting softly on the edge of the bed, she gently grabs the soft sex. She gave him a naughty look. He looked embarrassed.

"Relax!" She whispers!

Jack did not say a word, and tilted his head back. She drew her face closer to the penis, the contact of the skin with that of his client made him shiver. He liked her. She was aware of the childish panic that tormented her client. She knew that with this one, it would take patience.

A patience she willingly offered him: this gallant man was handsome, kind ... and above all, he could save her financially: she was several weeks late for her rent.

Mary Jane applied herself to her task, rubbed and cajoled tirelessly with all her expertise. After an hour of mad eroticism, the sleepy sexuality of the man slowly awoke. At the sight of his swollen penis, a mask of extraordinary relief passed over Jack's face. It gave him a feeling of liberation from a long imprisonment, full of the bliss of a prisoner who sees the light of day. Suddenly he let his instincts take over, and with the pretty prostitute he copulated until the complete satisfaction of his senses. He felt revived. Among the sweat and fluids, he did not stop taking it until four o'clock in the morning. Mary Jane Kelly turned to her partner: she had rarely seen such an expression of satiety. He looked at her; happy almost ingenuous and surprised at what he had just felt. She laughed sweetly, amused by the thrill of these animal games and the ecstasy they had provoked. She stared at him like an accomplice.

Suddenly Jack's changing eyes; became wicked. His smile disappeared. A transformation had suddenly taken place in Mister Hide; something dangerously bestial invaded him. Mary suddenly felt very frightened.

He lunged at her, and gripped her neck with his powerful hands.

"Oh murder!" She cries, in a voice stifled by Jack.

Too late, a red scarf was already wrapped around her neck and choked her throat with the strength of a python. Her mind did not understand the violence that sprang from this man, so tender an hour ago. Jack's technique was so smooth that in a dry motion, his kukri cut her carotid artery, and the blood spurted against the wall to the ceiling.

She lay there naked on the bed. Jack saw something else; a bundle of flesh that was all that remained of her; with its carnivorous matrix that had managed to devour his frustration. It did not haunt him now. In the darkness, seven years of misery danced around his victim's body, the last witness of his helplessness. He felt a new fire burning in him. He experienced a new epiphany, savouring this moment of intense mysticism where he found his splendour. The room was dark, like the devil's cave.

Still naked, he picked up old newspapers and clothes. He made them burn in a hellish fire, in the stove at the bottom of the room. The scene, lit by this diabolical light, was ready. He took his kukri and came back to the dead body. It was necessary to take the necessary samples. The best parts of her flesh were extracted with delicacy. Jack dug between Mary Jane's outstretched legs, pruning until the bone showed its whiteness.

He could not believe it: she was still beautiful, despite her gaping wounds, despite the bloody meat. He stabbed her face, and cut it out until he could see the skull between the slats of skin. When he saw it, he exulted; which doctor could come so close to the deformation of human flesh? Who could profane a body in such a way? (*)

Even Dante, in his visit to the infernal regions, had not seen such a spectacle. His hands entered the hole he had cleared; He removed the heart, which was still warm. His trophy; the heart which he bundled with a part of the uterus in a clean cloth.

The nightmare hour was coming to an end. He began to come back to his senses and got dressed. Without making any noise, he went out. As Kelly had done in front of him, he slid his arm through the broken tile of the window and quickly closed the lock. He was looking at his watch: five o'clock. He went quietly into Dorset Street. Hurrying, he took the path to the station. A little shiver of excitement ran through him: he carried away a part of the uterus and especially the heart of the most beautiful prostitute of London.

(*) Days of my Years - Melville Macnaghten 1914 p 60-61

14
Nº 13 Miller's Court; 10H 45

"Open, Kelly!"

Thomas Bowyer knocked against the door again. A loud and heavy sound resounded.

(*) The Star LONDON. SATURDAY, 10 NOVEMBER, 1888.
THE DISCOVERY OF THE BODY. This is how the discovery of the murder was made. …At a quarter to eleven yesterday morning, as the woman was 35s. In arrears with her rent, McCarthy said to a man employed by him in his shop, John Bowyer, "Go to No. 13 and try and get some rent."
He then tried the handle of the door and found it was locked. On looking through the keyhole he found THE KEY WAS MISSING.

"Kelly, I am coming for the rent! Mr McCarthy is sending me!"

No answer. No sign of life manifested itself. The ex-soldier paused, a little surprised that at a quarter to eleven he did not catch the prostitute at home. She was probably drinking the alcohol with the money she had made last night, and Thomas counted on following his boss's orders: the girl owed twenty nine shillings, several weeks in arrears.

Seeing that his efforts were unsuccessful, he approached the window without shutters. The window was broken. A thick curtain hid the inside of the room creating a minimum of protection against the cold. Thomas carefully passed his hand through the broken pane, and pulled the curtain aside. He was terrified when he discovered, looking inside the room, the horribly mutilated body on the bed. The sheets and mattress were red with blood. In horror, the ex soldier covered his eyes. He was a stout fellow with a thick moustache; but his composure was no longer sufficient to restrain his terror. He had seen horrible things during the war, but nothing that would have prepared him for this atrocious spectacle. He remained stunned for a moment. Recovering his spirits, he ran at full speed out of the yard, calling for help, shouting.

He quickly found Inspector Walter Beck, followed soon by Sergeant Edward Badham; to whom he recounted his horrible discovery, wild and feverish. The two policemen accompanied him to the spot straight away. Thomas pushed the fabric behind the window, the sergeant's face looking impassive. Years of crime had taught him to master himself, at least in appearance. The vision had left him very shaken, he became white and his sight was blurry. Inspector Beck had a little more trouble controlling him.

He took a step back when he saw the massacre, and a shiver of terror seized him, but he kept a respectable countenance. Thomas was livid. The two policemen, remembering their protective function of the citizens, made the greatest efforts to remain stoic.

All three men remained haunted by this frightful sight they had been the first to witness.

At 13:30, a large group of policemen was preparing to bring down the door of hell. Some police constables but many high ranking officers had reached the scene; Superintendent Thomas Arnold, Inspector Edmund Reid, Division H, Inspectors Frederick Abberline and Robert Anderson, accompanied by James Monro of Scotland Yard. Despite the general apprehension, everyone felt driven by a compelling curiosity; all knew that this murder was the worst of all.

The only one who was not present was Charles Warren!

Superintendent Arnold gave the signal for a PC, with the approval of the owner Mr. McCarthy, to smash the door of No. 13. With a few strikes of the pickaxe it broke. The policemen of the order entered the room; feeling nauseous more than one heart. A putrid smell suffocated the nostrils: it was the smell of blood oozing from the body.

It no longer looked human. The remains on the bed were spread out like shapeless pieces on a butcher's stall.

It was quickly noticed that a powerful fire had fed the stove. A simple observation showed that the murderer had used newspapers and the clothes of the victim, scattered in the room, to light the room. Only the last clothes Kelly had worn were neatly folded on the chair. The solder that connected the spout to the kettle had melted for the heat was too fierce. Abberline knew immediately that the killer had wanted more light. The only source of light Mary used in the room was a poor candle completely consumed.

"It was, a pretty girl" ... said a policeman in uniform.

Several inspectors reluctantly tried to reconstruct the scene that had taken place in this room. The ripper had enjoyed much more time than usual.

This proved the relentlessness with which he had disfigured the poor girl. In the street, he had only time to hit and disappear, here it was different, in a closed room, hidden from all, and he could give way to his basest instincts.

Superintendent Thomas Arnold gave orders to send a telegram to Sir Charles Warren to bring the two sleuth dogs, and a photographer to capture the scene of the crime.

The photographer arrived quickly at the beginning of the afternoon with his box and his tripod. When he put his camera back to the window, he put his head under his black cloth, which became, in the space of a pause, a veil of incongruous mourning.

He introduced a second sensitive plate into the chamber of his camera, changed the opening and pause time, and triggered the opening of the lens, his stopwatch.

Then the photographer moved his tripod to the end of the bed, against the wall and closed the curtains of the window to avoid a backlight. With a much longer break, for the third plate of sensitive glass, he took close ups of the horror... He folded his equipment and quickly left the room, he was livid.

Most of the inspectors were talking seriously, in a low voice. The first observations arose; the first deductions began to emerge. Abberline ordered the body to be taken for examination, disgusted in advance by the report of the autopsy he was going to read, for the search for leads.

A lot of pages of medical descriptions with a disgusting vocabulary; describing thoroughly the profanation that had soiled the blood-splattering room. How the tissues had been cut, what organs had been removed, what tortures had been inflicted ... Axphyxiated, Abberline went out to breathe some fresh air.

"I hope this time; Warren will deign to show himself!" In a stronger and more directive voice, he asked:

"Where are the two dogs Barnaby and Bhurgho?"

The demented spectacle in Mary Jane's room seemed to be gently infiltrated through the broken door; contaminating the city causing people to lose their heads.

Onlookers had already begun to congregate in Dorset Street, in front of the entrance to Miller's Court, and the police, in their confusion, had forgotten to cordon off the crime scene. The bloodhounds did not arrive. Warren did not arrive. Would Matthews act?

Charles Monro felt a sense of doom invading him. He already imagined the plethora of critics filling the newspapers. This crime was one atrocity too many! Something had just broken in the city; this fatal blow was going to inflame the people and the press against the Metropolitan Police of London. It was only a matter of time, before a great upheaval made the Yard shake to its foundations. (*)

(*) The Star LONDON. SATURDAY, 10 NOVEMBER, 1888.

James Monro hunts the ghost of Jack the Ripper

15

November, 1888 James Monro
takes up of Charles Warren's position

The Daily Telegraph decided to play the executioner's role this morning. Sir Charles Warren had qualities, of course, like kindness, gentleness, but these qualities seemed useless in the storm that was raging. In the streets, death was taunting the police, and the city needed a strong, strong man, not a slacker like Charles Warren. Warren was not alone aboard the failing ship, Matthews was the great helmsman. He had sailed carelessly, the sea was big, and when the waves began to break the deck, he realized that he could not control anything. A 'helpless impotence' wrote the journalists, wallowing in the pleonasm. The mistake was to have Matthews transferred from Whitehall to the House of Commons, and this error resulted in the appointment of the incompetent Charles Warren, who had been brought back from South Africa, to the post where he was only an embarrassment for Scotland Yard.

The Times denounced the fact that Londoners had been driven to a desperate situation. Matthews spoke in the House of Commons. He did not dwell on the reasons for James Monro's resignation on August 21, although these had a direct bearing on the problem. Regarding the elusive serial killer, it was not a failure of a new organization of the police, or a fault of the system. Matthews was trying to clear himself of responsibility for the decisions of his ministry, he was not wrong. In truth, his argument was correct: "The criminal displayed extraordinary cunning and diabolical discretion." Nobody could question that fact. This sad case had allowed the minister to consider the operation of the police as a whole; he could understand which improvements were necessary for the smooth running of Scotland Yard.

Only then did Matthews state in a clear and official voice that Sir Charles Warren resigned on November 8, 1888, and that it had been accepted by His Majesty's Government. The room applauds wildly. James Monro triumphed over Sir Charles Warren, and he would, encouraged by royal approval. The evening news only recalled the fact that Monro knew the Yard very well and that he had always continued to be a voice listened to by the ministry on the subject of police issues.

He was the best choice we could make.

The commissioner and the minister agreed and relations with the Criminal Investigation Division (CID) softened. It was not an easy task, but the newspapers cheered James Monro's return, expressing all their hopes, wishing him good luck. Above all, they hoped that Whitechapel's killer could be caught quickly. They were waiting for a man, a real man who, to succeed, had only one last thing to do: to forget politics, and to be only the servant of the city. This city full of swarming servants, craftsmen, workers, scoundrels ... where, in the middle of the crowd, a dangerous character was also lurking. The suspects were not lacking.

James Monro hunts the ghost of Jack the Ripper

16
December 1, 1888
John Druitt' suicide

Montague John Druitt was getting on his train to Charring Cross; he was in a hurry to get to Hammersmith, to meet the handsome Melville again.

Montague John Druitt

Outside the station, Druitt was getting closer to the Thames; he was walking along the riverbank, thinking of the past, which seemed to come back to him with each gust of wind.

He saw Windborne, the city where his father was the main surgeon. His gaze was thoughtful, as if he were immersed in a book. He did not look at the river. He saw pages, pages still turning, tirelessly, following a path that led him from Winchester College to the prestigious Oxford School.

John had chosen to study classical literature and law. His heart beat faster at this memory. The course of the river was like the thread of his life at that time: serene and inescapable. Entering the adult world, he obtained a post of teaching assistant in a boarding school in Blackheath for forty two very handsome boys.

The water of the river lapped oddly, for no reason. He had started playing cricket in Blackheath. Thanks to his talent, he had won a lot of trophies: Single titles, doubles, success, victory at the highest level. Then it was a whirlwind that had removed him from Blackheath. What had happened with these young boys to get him fired? These events, He wanted to forget those events.

The water became tumultuous.

He plunged back into the past, his law studies, and then some lucrative appearances at the bar, to deal with civil disputes.

During the days of freedom he had become a cricket pitcher. At the end of a match, he had met a big, broad shouldered fellow in the damp cloakroom. Sweat, two superb men with tough bodies. He was thinking again of Melville talking close to his shoulder, and the nice discussions!

"Did you play at Eton?"

"Indeed!" John Druitt shook his hand, with an undulating movement from his naked pectorals.

" I am genuinely amazed by your game." Said Melville.

"Thank you, we should play a game, one of these days."

"I have played in the same team as some of these gentlemen." Melville said.

"I suppose that's why you told me about Eton. Famous team! This explains your stature. Would you like to come and see me play at my next match?" I'll let you in, Druitt suggested.

"It will be a pleasure."

That's how Melville got closer to John. He attended games in which Druitt played.   (*)

(*) https://wikipedia / John Druitt.

Attention that satisfied the sportsman. At the end of the autumn; Melville Macnaghten offered John a meeting, one evening, on the quiet banks of the Thames.

And so it was that Druitt took his round-trip ticket Charing Cross - Hammersmith, this Saturday, December 1, the lover of literature headed to Chiswick with joy and excitement, for his rendezvous on the banks of the Thames. (*)

The first to arrive, watching the waves, he dreamt of, the imminent encounter with this handsome man. The wind caressed his throat like a soft scarf. The caress suddenly turned into a choking feeling. It was not the wind, but a piece of red stuff that had been wrapped around his neck! With a few gurgles, his inert body slumped at the foot of Jack.

The monster filled four big stones in each pocket of his victim, and dragged the body gently into the river. Montague John Druitt sank gently into the dark water, to reach the bottom of the Thames ... Jack was already far away.

(*) https://www.casebook.org/suspects/druitt.html.

17
December 15, 1888
James and Melville's joy

The Star Tavern was located right in the middle of Belgravia; just a few steps away from Buckingham Palace. A cozy place where a large chandelier lit up what looked more like a cozy living room than a drinking establishment. This is a place I knew well; it was a meeting point for members of respectable society and the working class. The atmosphere was jovial, smoky, and warm. Melville hailed me from a table near the fireplace.

"James! Over here, take a seat!"

He got up and shook my hand vigorously.

"Hey! You've eaten a lion, or should I say a leopard? "I said smiling.

"Ha! Please excuse my passion, I feel invigorated."

"My God! this is very good news! In all honesty, I found you, how to say ... Weakened, lately. You looked tired, weakened. It showed despite your best efforts."

It is quite true; I admit a sort of transient weakness. I suppose it was due to our return from India, which had destabilized me than it seems. I cannot explain why? Something I could not get rid of!

"I can not help wondering: how did this miraculous cure take place?"

Melville hesitated a moment.

"I can not explain it ... You are partly responsible!"

"Responsible?"

"Yes. Looking back, I realize that your visits and your invitations, your so faithful friendship, all that warmed my heart. You are a real friend! After my refusal for the job at Scotland Yard, for which you are not to blame, I felt quite disheartened. You were there to take me out of this hole! Everything rocked the night of the performance of Dr. Jekyll and Mr. Hyde, a real thunderclap!"

"Stop, I beg you, I only did what friends do! We have something to celebrate!"

"To celebrate? I am interested."

Melville motioned to the charming twenty year old waitress of about twenty to come and take the order.

She had a graceful figure. Melville, with an assurance that I had not seen in him for a long time, welcomed the young nymph like a perfect gentleman.

"Serve us two glasses of your best ginger beer" he said with the negligence of a master.

The girl smiles, lowers her eyes, and murmured "I'll be quick" who made her delicate face blush. The waitress came back with our beers, which she placed on the table.

"Well," said Melville. "What are we to celebrate?"

"My dear fellow, I must remind you of certain facts. Do you allow me to be boring for a few moments?"

"I'll allow you anything you want. You are never boring."

"I'll be quick. As you know, the one that prevented me from keeping the promise that I made to you to return to Scotland Yard resigned at the time of the murder of Dorset Street. I immediately applied to replace him. The entire Yard had already supported me for a long time, and the very next day I was congratulated by my troops. I officially took office on December 3, 1888 to replace Charles Warren."

"It's fantastic!" Exclaims Melville

The waitress came back with our beers, which she put on the table. My friend, all smiles, realized what was going on.

"Absolutely! The most fantastic thing is that I'm going to make you join our metropolitan force." I said with a wink.

We drank laughing. (*)

(*) Morning Advertiser (London) 3 December 1888

Mr. Monro, the new commissioner of the metropolitan police, will, we understand, commence his duties at Whitehall-place to-day, and henceforth his signature will replace that of Sir Charles Warren on all police orders. Since his resignation from the post of Assistant Commissioner, Mr Monro has been in attendance at the Home Office almost daily.

18
Monday, December 24, 1888
Ovingdean House; the father's death

East of Brighton; Ovingdean House's beautiful residence was immersed in a cold, white atmosphere. The Macnaghten clan had converged on the family home, and in the last few days all had found themselves between the thick walls that contained thirteen rooms.

The warm hearth of the chimney in the main salon incited laziness, and almost all the Macnaghten spent long hours there. The living room was large; it was well arranged for adults to rest and children to play.

The festivities were being prepared by the servants who were busy cooking and attending to fifteen family members.

The patriarch and master of the place; Sir Elliot Macnaghten always showed himself in an unpleasant mood; grumpy and irascible. His authority was felt in every room where he was, it hovered, menacing and silent. From the back of an armchair, he scanned the guests with a dark eye, like a great raptor, who occasionally opened his mouth to utter an order. When we listened, all the joy in the home seemed to disappear. The little ones stopped their games abruptly, the big ones raised their eyes from their book, and others put down their glasses. Elliot Macnagthen appreciated his power, and nothing pleased him more than to use it, like a monarch in his castle.

Upon the arrival of Melville and his wife and children, Elliot did not fail to be sarcastic. They were late. On the steps, he remained silent, smiled at the children with the goodness of a grandfather, took the hand of his daughter-in-law, and led her into the house with the delicacy of a man of the world. Not a look, not a word for his son. Melville said nothing, knowing that an angry look satisfied his father. At the table, Melville was talking about the play he had just seen in London.

"You are still passionate about your childhood fantasies!"

An embarrassing silence fell on the table. No one dared to help Melville escape the perpetual reprimands he was subjected to. Elliot, though old, aroused a fear that was difficult to overcome.

"I know that my passion hardly moves you, Father."

"A passion! Just a fad! I still remember the day you came to see me with an eager look: "Father! I want to be an actor. You are still as crazy as ever."

"You did not hesitate to tell me!"

Lightning flashed from Elliot's eyes. The answer was arrogant, and the father made it clear to his son. With a threatening owl's eye, he showed him that he had better keep his mouth shut, if he did not want to be ridiculed in public. The meal was resumed only once the master of the house put his fork back to his mouth.

What could fuel so much hatred from the father? No one knew it. At teatime, the tension went up a notch. Melville was discussing India with his wife and cousin, in the bantering tone of the most mundane conversation.

"Still a pretty waste of time" says Elliot.

"I beg your pardon?"

"You understood me very well. What good did you ever do in India, except hitting your head?"

"Is not this the truth?" Not even able to gain respect from three chewers of betel leaves. Even your wife I had to find for you. This time Melville turned red. His blond moustache was paling, his eyes widened, his fists clenched. With an incredible mastery of himself he stood up calmly and answered in a toneless voice:

"I am leaving in a few moments."

And he did it.

"Yes, go out. You are good at running away!"

A nasty smile distorted Elliot's ruthless face; he triumphed. Dora was paralysed with shame but her good manners prevented her from showing her feelings. The behaviour of the father was odious, few explained it to him, and none had the audacity to intervene and to stop these endless reproaches. Even this feast of the birth of Christ was not enough to appease the two men, let alone make them forgive each other. Christmas Eve was traditional; we ate and drank a lot, then each family retired to their room.

Elliot was satiated, he was lying in his bed with a full stomach, waiting for sleep. In his warm drowsiness, he gazed at the hearth of his room. Sometimes a figure seemed to slip on the wall, a figment of his imagination.

162

The last crackling of the fire reminded him of the fire of his warehouses, that dreadful Thursday, August 30, 1888. The heat made him sweat on the surface of his body. He thought of his son, the position he had the magnanimity to secure for him. Once again, his thoughts lingered on the docks, making their way from the warehouses to the fire. The premises of the dream were heavy on his conscience. He had the impression that Melville was standing right in front of him, at the foot of his bed. The dream became more powerful: Melville accused himself of the destruction of the warehouses of the East India Company, with tears of anger in his eyes. Elliot mumbled something, but the feeling of warmth in the room and its heaviness choked him. He felt unable to move. He was looking at the ceiling, which was distorted by the light coming from the chimney and then blackness surrounded him.

The following morning, on Christmas day, the uncontrolled shrieks of a servant alerted the household.

There was no time for joy anymore. Elliot Macnagthen lay in bed, mouth open. He was dead. (*)

James Monro hunts the ghost of Jack the Ripper

19
Monday, June 3, 1889
Early days at the Yard

Since November 10, 1888, the murders perpetrated by the so-called "Jack the Ripper" seemed to have stopped. The police were inundated with anonymous letters, examining in detail all the suicides and internments in psychiatric asylum. All the assumptions about possible suspects were considered.

What was becoming of "Jack the Ripper"? On the 31st, a boatman pulled a very elegant man from the Thames. PC George Moulson found four large stones in each pocket of his suit, a pair of gloves, a watch with a gold chain, an unused Hammersmith / Charring Cross return ticket, and a white handkerchief stained with mud. (*)

Scotland Yard, who was investigating this death, identified this man as Montague John Druitt. His homosexual past was discovered, as well as his dismissal from the post of teaching assistant at Blackheath Boys' School.

(*) https://www.casebook.org/suspects/druitt.html.

The killings of Jack the Ripper had ceased since the discovery of this drowned man, so the police supposed he could be the wanted murderer. James Monro asked for this drowning of the Thames, to be treated as a suicide. The police decreed that Jack the Ripper had committed suicide and that it was now forbidden for the press to continue to make headlines on this case ... A short time later, James Monro obtained from Minister Mattews, the appointment of Melville Macnaghten, as Chief Assistant to Mr Robert Anderson at Scotland Yard. Melville entered the Yard on June 1, 1889, and was immediately confronted with his first murder case.

A mutilated body; but not disembowelled whose remains are found scattered on the banks of the Thames. Melville assisted by his officer in charge of the investigation, went to the crime scene. A scar on one of her wrists led to the identification of a woman, Elizabeth Jackson. A builder, who had been seen in her company, was suspected. But he had an irrefutable alibi and was quickly released.

This sordid affair became "the mystery of the Thames", a file that remained unsolved.

20
End of June 1889
PC James Harvey meets James Monro

On a beautiful afternoon in late June, there was a knock on my door. I knew that PC James Harvey had requested an interview.

"Come in."

PC Harvey entered the office, intimidated, stammering an almost imperceptible greeting, in what seemed like a crucial moment to him.

"Sit down, Harvey, take a seat "

"Thank you Sir."

"Very good. Tell me what brings you here, Harvey, I'm listening to you."

The PC was trying to hide his worries behind an imperturbable mask. His countenance was that of a police officer, but his eyes showed a lingering anxiety.

"Sir. It's about Anderson's new assistant."

"Macnagthen?" Asked Monro

Harvey hesitated...

"Do you remember the killings of Jack the Ripper?"

I looked at him, perplexed.

"Of course I do. Everyone remembers them."

"Yes Sir, forgive me, but..."

"Speak Harvey! I'm listening to you!"

"During that woman's murder, Catherine Eddowes in Mitre Square in September. I met a man on Duke Street during my round."

"I remember it's in the report..."

"That man! Well! I've just seen him here again; he's the new assistant to the chief of police; it's assistant Macnaghten."

For a moment I was stunned and during that second I remembered the offices of Kearley&Tongue in Mitre Square... the tiny square. I thought of the access to the offices and in a flash everything was explained; here was the famous hiding place in which the killer could easily enter Kearley & Tonge and leave quietly under the police's nose. Obviously Macnaghten would have had no problem entering and hiding because he knew the place by heart and was aware of the habits of its security guard Morris.

Now I remembered that Harvey on duty in the north must have seen the killer on Duke Street; along with Lawende and his two friends coming out of the Emperor's Club. They had reported coming across that man.

And now this chance meeting had occurred in Scotland Yard. PC Harvey had met Melville Macnaghten.

I thought back to little scenes from the past; Melville's tortured gaze his fascination with Dr. Jekyll and Mister Hyde's play.

His passion, his troubles during that dinner at home, his hunting memories. It might seem futile but in fact everything fitted into place. These minute details came back to me, and I kept repeating to me "Melville is the killer. My friend Melville..." Despite these ideas that assailed me, my first reaction was immediate:

"It's not possible Harvey!"

"But Sir..."

"Strictly impossible! It reminds me that you PC Harvey; you should have returned to Mitre Square at the exact moment during which the murderer was committing his crime. I remember it very well. At the same time PC Edward Watkins was coming from the south; through Mitre Street. Is it right; Harvey? The man could only go out by Church Passage where you were supposed to do your round."

"I remember it very well indeed. What were you doing at that time?"

"Chief," stammered James Harvey who did not understand anything.

The policeman had entered my office with vital information to confide to me and he was being chided for his careless behaviour more than eight months ago. My reaction caught him off guard. I took advantage of his surprise to ascertain my position.

"Mister Macnaghten is irreproachable. As for you! I suggest you to do fewer rounds in pubs. Now leave my office at once!"

Stunned, the policeman stood up silently, with a blank look on his face. He took his leave.

"When you go you will ask my secretary too come because from now you are no longer a member of the police, Harvey!"

He nodded respectfully, in spite of the ringing in his ears, and then took a hasty step. Moments later the secretary knocked on the door.

"Did you ask for me, Sir?"

"Please make a note of this: dismiss PC Harvey without giving a cause.

Give this message to anyone who needs to be aware of this."

Document indicating the dismissal of PC Harvey
without any reason indicated.

James Monro hunts the ghost of Jack the Ripper

21
October, 1889
Meeting between Melville and James Monro

Although the street was crowded, the backyard was empty and unobtrusive. I was waiting for Melville and the more I waited; the more nervous I felt. Since PC Harvey's visit to my office; I had gone back to investigating Jack the Ripper. I could not believe it. My friend... my good friend Melville! What legion of demons was devouring him now?

I had read all the reports. I could not keep the problem out of my mind, I had examined everything from every angle, and I had to accept this fact: Melville was the man that PC Harvey had spotted that day and that man could only be the killer, whom he and I had nicknamed Nemo. Now it was my deepest belief. The proximity of the offices where Melville worked was just confirmed my suspicions. My information had confirmed to me that Kearley & Tonge's guard; Mr George Morris usually sat every night in Mitre Square.

Except every Saturday when he cleaned the accounts offices opposite the place in the second building of Kearley & Tonge ... and precisely the twenty ninth of September was a Saturday. I looked at my watch. Melville did not arrive. Crazy ideas and irrational theories were beginning to form in my mind, adding to my confusion. Would my friend on hearing what I was going to say to him, throw myself at me, and slaughter me like one of those victims? "Why did you bring me to this lost corner of town, my friend?"

Immersed in my thoughts, I was startled. Melville was staring at me, looking surprised. He had touched my shoulder. While dusting myself, I noted this sudden familiarity. He had never done this to me before. I spoke again.

"Melville, I have to talk to you about something very important."

"That's what your ticket says."

"Yes, it is vital that we speak in a secret place."

"This place is perfect. I'm listening to you! What is this important case?"

"Good. I will be direct. The day the ripper killed two people; that night a witness named Lawende saw a man a man with the woman Eddowes at the corner of Duke Street and Church Passage. He had already come across this man, because he works next to Kearley & Tonge."

Strangely, Melville kept silent. He was staring straight at me; attentive with no detectable movement on his face; except a strange veil of harshness when I said the words Kearley & Tonge. Not wanting to display his emotions, he did not move an inch; an attitude that made me hides my nervousness. My training in the Army helped me to stand up straight.

"At the end of June, at the Yard, PC James Harvey asked to see me. He wanted to tell me that he too had met and even greeted a man on Duke Street. The day of Eddowes' murder!"

"Harwey saw this man at Scotland Yard running in the corridors. He told me this man is the new assistant to Commissioner Robert Anderson. I was talking with confidence, without faltering." At this moment I was seeing Nemo right in front of me. I did not know if it was the revelation I had just made to him that reminded me of that! He had not changed his posture; not an inch. A kind of fire had just lit up in the depths of his pupils. A fire full of sulphur; a devouring fire; it was the look of a predator. A leopard, I could have sworn at that moment. No sound came out of his mouth; and we remained silent and paralyzed for a long time. I had to keep my composure in front of the beast without weakening.

"I will not insult you by adding any more. It's useless after this revelation."

"I could not believe it: I dismissed the PC Harvey from his functions on the spot. I prevented Joseph Lawende from giving a description of the character in court; that was with Eddowes; at the corner of Church Pass. He looked too much like you." The silence was a real torture, Melville knew it only too well and he was silent. I could not help asking him.

"Melville ... Why?"

"To cause Charles Warren's downfall." He replied coldly.

"Make Charles Warren fall, by murdering five prostitutes?"

"I wanted you to take his place; it's obvious!"

He spoke in a very casual tone which terrified me. He continued, very seriously, his explanations, with a mad fever:

"It was necessary to act, to discredit Warren to the population. These women belonged to the dregs of society prostitutes whom these gentlemen were going to see, and who were hiding from the police. You know it very well. You are a policeman. Whitechapel is where decent people cheat on their wives. It's even easier than elsewhere. That's right, I admit, I took the opportunity to also solve my famous problems, which we had already discussed, in the evening we watched "Dr Jekyll and Mister Hyde", do you remember?"

More calmly he went on.

"If you knew how many years it took me to solve them... Seven long years! But I finally got there. And finally I was able to heal myself. Thanks to you, I can now fully satisfy my wife. My brain has found complete serenity, just like before May 1881 and I am sure a third birth will soon complete my family." (*)

He was there in flesh and blood before me; talking quietly about his new happiness. At a swift pace, the madness that had swept away my friend was before me. I felt like I was at the theatre and Melville, passionate as always played a role inspired by what we had seen. Nothing in him revealed the slightest aggressiveness. He had just told me the truth; justifying himself as one justifies a point of rule in cricket. He looked at me for a long time. It was clear that he was waiting for my reaction, and that he was ready to judge me should the need arise. His moustache gave him a feline look, a kind of metamorphosis was taking place in front of my eyes, and it became frightening.

(*) Days of my Years - Melville Macnaghten 1914 p 62

Fear was invading me. The story was going too far, it was I who had begged Minister Henry Matthews for Melville to join Scotland Yard, against the advice of Charles Warren; I had fired PC Harvey and protected Melville by preventing Lawende from testifying.

I could not go back without causing an earthquake that would annihilate my family, but also Dora and her children.

"I would not say that, Melville! Do not doubt it!"

Melville's gaze softened, he smiled and took my arm, gentle, polite but scary.

"What are we doing here now, my dear?"

22
June, 1890
Monro resigns from the Yard and returns to India

The months following our meeting were very difficult, I kept looking at the files but the facts were overwhelming, I took notes and I began writing a report. Working at Scotland Yard, having to work with Melville was becoming unbearable. I had not hesitated to resign on June 10, 1890. Two years after the murders, and Melville's revelations, I had taken advantage of the Minister's refusal to increase the Police pensions. The decision took effect on June 20, 1890. I had to be as discreet as possible and protect Melville's reputation. The pension business was not something to be taken lightly. In fact, it underlined my dissensions with Sir Charles Warren. The context in which the murders took place is not to be minimized.

Long before Melville made his appearance in England, Warren already wanted to control my actions and my dealings with the department. He wanted me to inform him of any mail exchanged.

He did not understand that although my position included the term assistant, I was in no way a subordinate. In terms of appointments, I was not accountable to him. I had told my friend Melville that he had been accepted as Deputy Chief of Police, he had then come from the other side of the earth to undertake his new function.

After Melville's return, Warren had changed his mind; I had, however, sworn to help him. I had then proposed my resignation, which had been accepted. That's where our four-penny war had led us. As for me, I did not stop; I remained firmly attached to my convictions. I had the support of my men and the press. Subsequently I was presented with a bill on pension reform so much hoped for my men; I approved it with the satisfaction of a well fought battle. When the House of Commons voted a simplified version of the retirement plan, I jumped at the opportunity to escape with my heavy secret and resign. (*)

(*) https://en.wikipedia.org/wiki/James_Monro

July 18th was to be my new starting point, an evening meeting of which I was the honorary president. All my colleagues, all my superiors, everybody including Melville attended. They had approved me, congratulated me, transformed me... It was a fact; I was appreciated by my peers, but also by the press. It was the last act, the one where I disappeared, taking with me the painful secret of Jack the Ripper.

I was returning with a wife and children to India on a medical mission to Rhanagat; forty miles north of Calcutta. (*)

A humanitarian job without remuneration; chosen to atone for my sins.

Quickly I took my pen to transcribe all my notes about the murders in a very detailed manner, in a highly private memorandum. I wanted to leave a trace for my family.

The following days I wrote the:

'Highly private memorandum'

Melville was violently hit on the head in May 1881 in Kishnaghur; he lost his libido and could no longer satisfy his wife Dora. His family was limited to two children and he and his wife lived seven years without having intercourse.

(*) https://www.revolvy.com/page/James-Monro?source=folders

Melville returned to London in May 1888; to take a police position granted by Charles Warren on March 29, 1888. He is not known to anybody and can therefore circulate in London without being recognized by anyone.

The reversal of fortune in early April, with Charles Warren's refusal to give Melville the position of police officer, led to intense frustration in Melville's sick mind. It reawakened his hatred towards his father who had prevented him from becoming an actor.

Charles Warren had deprived him of the position he had hoped for and which would have allowed him to show his father that he could manage without him.

1°) for this reason, on August 30, 1888, the first thing Melville did was set fire to the 'Warehouses of the Indian Company' which belonged to his father Elliot Macnaghten. He had already prepared his diabolical plan since he immediately murdered his first victim; Mary Ann Nichols in Buck's Row; near Kearley & Co's office in Thomas street. He had the keys to access one of his two offices after his rampage.

2 °) Then we have the second murder on Saturday, September 8, 1888, he murdered Annie Chapman in the inner courtyard of 29 Hanbury Street; which allowed him to take the uterus of his victim, he devoured it in an act of madness to try to solve his impotence.

3 °) Saturday, September 29, 1888, he murdered Elisabeth Stride, but witnesses leaving the club of Jewish Socialists, and a cart led by Louis Diemschutz disrupted the madman's plans.

Melville, who had already strangled and slaughtered his victim, fled to Duke Street where he met PC James Harvey who was doing his usual round.

He approached Catherine Eddowes and chatted with her at the corner of Duke Street and Church Passage at which point Lawende and his two friends were able to make a precise description of Melville. Man of 30/35 years, height 1 meter 75, light complexion with a large build, blond moustache, red handkerchief tied around his neck, and wearing a dark cloth cap with a visor of the same colour; giving him the appearance of a sailor; wearing a long gray coat of shabby appearance.

Melville murdered his second victim in a corner of Mitre Square, in a dark area, he had sabotaged the day before the gas lamp that lit up the place. Again he took the uterus of his victim, but also the left kidney, and a half-apron covered with blood, to carry his trophies.

4 °) In the Kearley & Tonge building; more than an hour later he swapped his sailor's disguise for his usual clothes. He took half of Catherine Eddowes' apron as well as a piece of chalk lying next to his blackboard, and quietly came out of Kearley & Tonge.

He walked halfway from his first crime to reach 119 Goulston Street. He deposited the piece of apron there in front of a dark wall on which he inscribed with his chalk: "The Juwes are the men that will not be blamed for nothing" His aim was obviously to prove that the two crimes had been committed by the same hand.

(5) Later, Melville sent half a kidney to Whitechapel Vigilante Committee chairman George Lusk, accompanied by the letter 'From Hell'; confirming that he had devoured the other half of the kidney and that in addition it was very good.

6 °) November 9, Melville had a sexual relationship with Marie Jane Kelly; a young and pretty 25 year old prostitute. He savagely murdered her and, for the third time, removed part of the uterus but also the heart of his victim which he later devoured in an attempt to regain his manhood for good.

7 °) The first of June 1889; Melville Macnaghten becomes the assistant to the chief of the police; and begins to work. PC Harvey comes across him in the corridor and recognises him.

PC 964 James Harvey is immediately fired from the police.

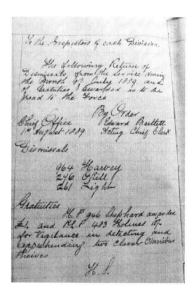

James Monro hunts the ghost of Jack the Ripper

23
December 1890
Christabel Mary Melville Macnaghten

After the crimes Melville and Dora were able to resume a satisfactory sex life, and on December 9, 1890, Dora gave birth to Christabel Mary, to the delight of her proud father. It was proof of their new found love.

Two years after the family event, Macnaghten had moved away from their friend Oscar Wilde who came into trouble because of his homosexuality.

One Sunday, Melville took his ten year old daughter to Scotland Yard where he was working on an urgent case.

Opening her daddy's drawers, Christabel came across a file with photographs of the naked and mutilated bodies Jack the Ripper's victims. The shock was terrible for the little girl, and her father leaped up to close the album with a deeply concerned face.

A few years later Christabel became a beautiful young girl, dating young men under the close supervision of her worried parents.

But those happy times were short lived for Christabel. In 1910, Melville decided to marry his daughter to Henri McLaren, the son of a prominent English aristocratic family. A prestigious wedding was organized on July 19, 1910.

Sir Melville Macnaghten marie sa fille
Christabel Mary le 19 juillet 1910

Ten months later, on May 31, 1911, Christabel gave birth to a little girl, Elizabeth Mary Mc Laren.

Some time after her marriage, her mother Dora confided in her that she was the child of the newfound love.

This startling statement took Christabel by surprise off her feet, and then she came to her senses, finally persuading her mother to tell her the truth about "who her father really was" and why her friends were asking her for details about Jack the Ripper's misdeeds.

But her mother explained to her that her elder brother and sister were born in India in the first two years of their marriage; that they had to be sent back to England when they were still very young, and so she and her father had decided not to have any more children. But when Melville was offered a job at Scotland Yard eight year later, they realised that what they wanted most in the world was another child. (*)

This marriage to a large English aristocratic family allowed Melville Macnaghten to permanently bury the terrible secret kept by Scotland Yard.

(*) A wiser Woman? A book of Memories /

Christabel Aberconway McLaren edited Hutchinson and Co LTD 1966.

James Monro hunts the ghost of Jack the Ripper

Afterword

The last years of Melville Macnaghten:

* Entered Scotland Yard on June 1, 1889 with the help of James Monro, Melville became Deputy Commissioner (CID).

* On December 29, 1903, he succeeded Edward Bradfort as assistant commissioner head of the Belper committee, in charge of criminal identification (fingerprinting), and in 1905 was the first deputy commissioner who identified a culprit, Alfred Stratton, guilty of robbery and murder, by taking a fingerprint off the material underneath the cash register.

* Melville Macnaghten was decorated in 1907 by King Edward VII for his service to the British Crown; he was appointed Commander of the Order of the British Empire.

* In 1912 he became a companion of the "Order of Bath".

* In 1913 he received the King's Police Medal. He was also elevated to the title of Commander of the White Military Order of Spain and the Order of the Dannebrog.

* In 1911, his headaches, caused by the blow to his head sustained in 1881, worsened the upper hand and despite a trip to Australia the whole year was unbearable and he retired from the police in 1913

* In 1914 Sir Melville Macnaghten writes his memoirs "Days of My Years": Editions: London, Edward Arnold

New York, Longmans, Green & Co.

* Sir Melville Macnaghten **dies on May 12, 1921** at Queen's Anne's House in Westminster.

Pall Mall Gazette on Tuesday, March 31, 1903

Sims the Pall Mall Gazette reporter visited Mr F.G. Abberline, Former Chief Detective Inspector of Scotland Yard.

Frederick Abberline says:

"It is certain that Whitechapel's murderer (Jack the Ripper) has long been known to be beyond the reach of earthly justice."

:

"You can say most emphatically," said Mr Abberline, "Scotland Yard is really no wiser on this point than it was fifteen years ago.

It is simply absurd to say that the police have proof that the man is dead.

I am and always have been in close contact with Scotland Yard, and it would have been almost impossible for me not to know everything about it.

Moreover, the authorities would have been only too happy to put an end to

such a mystery, if only for their own credit. "

By Nigel Morland sometime in the 1925's
Reported in the 'Evening News' 26/6/1976

I visited Abberline when he was living in retirement in
Dorset.
In spite of my efforts he was very cagey and said he had no
intention of discussing the case in detail. He was sick of the
whole business. But when I mentioned two friends of mine
– Edgar Wallace and Henry Battley, who became Chief
Inspector of the fingerprint bureau – he relented a little.

The case, he said, was tightly shut. "I've given my word to
keep my mouth permanently closed about it."
But he let slip some revealing comments.
"There was a lot of material never entered in any records," he
said. "Here say stuff, word-of-mouth information and orders
in 1888-9 to forget all about the affair."

"Then neither you nor anyone else knows who the Ripper
was?" as I was ushered firmly out of the house.
"I know," he said, "and my superiors know certain facts."
He was not going to give the details to me or anyone else.
But he added, and I remember distinctly his exact words:
"It wasn't a butcher, Yid or foreign skipper, as he was
supposed to be ... you'd have to look for him not at the
bottom of London society at the time, but a long way up.
That's all I will ever say. Goodbye."

And the door was firmly closed.

James Monro hunts the ghost of Jack the Ripper

Attachments

I. The memorandum written by Macnaghten in 1894

Summary:

The Star at the beginning of 1894 accused Thomas Cutbush of being Jack the Ripper. But Thomas was a relative of Superintendent Charles Henry Cutbush; so Minister Henry Mattews asked a police officer to produce a memorandum detailing the Yard's observations on the subject. Melville Macnaghten was in charge of the writing.

Melville put forward a theory suggesting the murderer could be ambidextrous, recalled the five murders, the five victims, the way they had been killed (with strong descriptions and adjectives), lingered on the last murder, mentioned the "infernal character" of this ritual killing, almost praising the inconceivable brutality of the massacre. Curiously, the article dwelt on the double murder of September 30th. The paragraph was a logical continuation of the previous one, with strong insistence on the violence, the mutilations, the fury of the murderer in an almost obsessive way.

Then, giving his opinion as to why the crimes had suddenly ceased, Melville once again emphasized the importance on the bloody catharsis of the fifth and ultimate killing. An excess so terrible that it had pushed the killer to commit suicide or be interned in a lunatic asylum.

A final way to bury Nemo. Not without malice, he recalled that PC Harvey who was in Duke Street on the night of Catherine Eddowes' murder, was the only PC who had had a good look at the killer, but without being able to give a precise description of him. After this statement, the memo dwelt on the potential suspects: Melville was adamant that there were only three strong suspects: **Druitt,** Kominsky, and Ostrog. He was convinced that **Druitt was the culprit**. But according to him; the truth would never be known.

Druitt lay "**like a lie at the bottom of the Thames**".

Melville ended his Memorandum by confirming that the crimes of recent years could not have been committed by Thomas Cutbush.

Let's put together the last sentences written by Macnaghten:

"**The truth** will never be known, **Druitt is like a lie** at the **bottom of the Thames**".

We found the 2 versions of this memorandum and the From Hell letter:

1 °) The whole of the handwritten version of the draft Memorandum written by Melville Macnaghten was held by the eldest daughter Julia Mary Donner; and given at the end of its life to his sister Lady Christabel; who copied in 1938 the machine to write the draft of his father in 7 typewritten pages; forgetting in the middle of page 6 the two pages written by his father that she will keep at the end of the document. These are the two handwritten pages "6A" and "6B" which Lady Christabel would have forgotten to insert in her copy. On her work she wrote the first handwritten mention 'By my father Sir MM-', and in the middle of page 6 she indicated in pencil that she had to insert the two handwritten pages of her father 'memo 6A' and 'memo 6B' Which are the relics of the first full version written by his father. This complete document was made public by Christopher Melville McLaren (Lady Christabel's fifth child) in 1986; and confirmed by letter on November 24, 2010.

2 °) pages 1 to 7 of the confidential "final memorandum", handwritten by Melville Macnaghten and given to Scotland Yard in 1894. This memorandum is in the UK National Archives [MEPO 3/141, ff. 177-183]. And circulates on the net in a "PDF" document of 7 pages.

The first page is marked "Confidential" at the top left, and features Melville Macnaghten's personal round pad. The 7th page of the document signed by Melville Macnaghten is dated February 23, 1894.

3) Anonymous handwritten letter "From hell" with a blood red outline addressed on 16 October 1888; with Catherine Eddowes's half-kidney; to "Mister Lusk".

4 °) Copy of the two signatures of Melville Macnaghten taken on his Memorandum of 1894 and on his book "Days of my Years" of 1914

Signature on the confidential memo of 1894

Signature on his book
'Days of my Years' from 1914

II. The mystery of the writing of
Sir Melville Leslie Macnaghten (1853-1921)

This study was carried out on the following digitized documents; which one is unaware of the formats:

— pages 1 and 7 of the "typed memorandum" on which appear of the handwritten mentions probably written in the mine graphite (lead pencil)

— Two handwritten layers by Melville Macnaghten headings "memorandum 6A" and "memorandum 6B"; probably written with black ink, seven handwritten layers of the "final memorandum",

— The handwritten anonymous letter "From Hell", addressed to "Mr. Lusk", the red layout blood.

Typed memorandum – beginning of the page

This document typed by the entourage of Melville Macnaghten is the reproduction of the first handwritten version of a memorandum disappeared to date.

It is the counterpart, with the corrections carried out, of the handwritten final memorandum given to the police on February 23rd, 1894 by Melville Macnaghten.

Final memorandum, manuscript given to the police
(The first five lines)

The typed memorandum was supplemented by the notes of the 6A pages and 6B, as indicated in the partly central lead pencil of its page 6 and to the bottom of the handwritten memo 6B.

Obviously, the mention ` by my father Sir M.M – ` was written by Christabel daughter of Melville Macnaghten.

Typed memorandum – central part of page 6

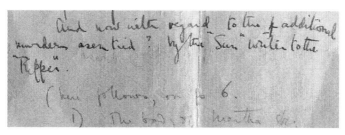

Memo 6B with black ink,

with annotations (lead pencil).

The writing of the "final memorandum", neat and regularly tilted, is of conventional style suitable for the 19th century. This writing is disciplined much than the writing with black ink and the lead pencil of the "memos 6A and 6B" animated by more movement and oscillations around the vertical. By bringing the writing closer to the "final memorandum" with that with black ink 6A and 6B, one discovers a certain number of similarities between regularly tilted graphics and the more alive writing with black ink, so much as regards the ordinance (inequalities of the line spaces more tightened on the left than on the right forming lines in "range", more or less large sinuosity of the lines, end of falling lines, indent instead of full stop, slightly nearer to the last word of the sentence than of the first word of the following sentence, which is as the case of the commas) as methods of connections and finales.

Illustrations:

Final Memorandum

Line spaces in range, more tightened on the left than on the right, with ends of falling lines

Memo 6A, line 16 and 17

Memo final   Memo 6A line 15

Full stop replaced by an indent, centered in space separating the last word from the sentence, the first word of the following sentence. To also note, on both sides, the connection in arcade between "O" and "N" of "one".

Alternation of concave and convex connections between "O" and "F

On both sides, presence of 'r' calligraphic magnifying
on "Public garden" and "murder"
as well as finales bent towards the left

Apart from at the very least obvious differences in slope,
there into force exist other divergences on the level of the
jambs of "G", "p", "Q" and "there", open on the left in the
writing regularly tilted in accordance with penmanship at the
time, and open on the line in the unequal writing to the black
ink, more released of the calligraphic constraints.

Memorandum final   Memo 6B, line 9 at 11

The enumeration of the resemblances and the
dissimilarities is far from being exhaustive. How are they
explained?   They are quite simply significant of an
ambidextrous. To write; an ambidexterity makes use as well
of his right hand as of his left hand. Some have a preferential
hand, others not. It acts, in fact, of a natural capacity offered
by the brain.

Frequently, especially when it acts script writers provided education for before 1960, the writing of the right hand is of slope inclined, contrary to that of the left hand, more rectified or more unequal, at least concerning the Latin writings.

In a current way, one of the writings is structured than the other, often also more calligraphic. The arcades appear indifferently in the writing of the right hand and the left hand. But whatever the case of figure, beyond the differences related to reversed control of the gesture, it does not matter the hand used, the ordinance of the text (margins, line spaces, spaces between the words) is similar. The two writings also sharing the same automatisms, i.e. of the characteristics specific to the script writer, which are often in the attacks, the finales, the accents, the points on "I", the commas, certain connections, etc On the other hand, one rather regularly notes differences in direction on the level of certain jambs and/or finales. In some rare cases, there exists a perfect agreement between the writing of the right hand and that of the left hand. Mainly, more the writing is personalized; more the differences between the writings of the right hand and of the left hand are accentuated. Contrary, when the writing remains dependent on the taught model and that it engages with difficulty in progressiveness, the variations are attenuated by slowness related to the lack of practice.

As most script writers with plurality of writings, Melville Macnaghten books his calligraphic writing (regularly tilted writing) with initial carefully drawn with the foreign trade (final memorandum given to the police), this at the same time to be readable and to run themselves in the mould of suitability, but also to give a good image of oneself and to thus attract the external recognition, whereas it keeps for him the more unequal, more spread out and more spontaneous writing of the memos 6A and 6B written for him.

We interest now in the anonymous handwritten letter coming from the hell "From hell", addressed on October 16th, 1888 to Mr. Lusk.

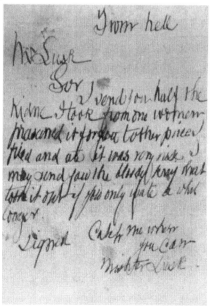

We note that graphics close to taught penmanship more constrained, is slowed down more and more excessive in its dimensions and forms at the beginning of text that towards the end. This is typical disguised writing used to prevent the identification, where the starting application is slackened progressively, quite simply because the script writer concentrates more on the contents of his missive, to the detriment of the attention related to the form of graphics. It can carry out both of face with difficulty.

When one compares the writing of this anonymous letter with those of the letters of reference allotted to Sir Melville Macnaghten, one belongs to obvious variations to put on disguise of the writing, exaggerated in his dimension, his tightening, his forms and certain proportions.

A more attentive observation however reveals common points in the page layout, on the level of the interpellation "Sir" located below left edge of the text at the image of the last paragraph of the handwritten layer 6B, of the instability of the axes and the lines, the tangles equivalent to those of the layers 6A and B, of the indent on the right of "Mister Lusk" of the last line, agreeing with that which follows the authentic signature of Melville Macnaghten.

As regards automatisms reproduced with length of time and without at all being aware from it, these elements escape control completely from the script writer.

 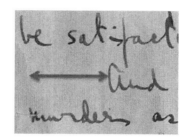

Memo 6B line 17 and 18

Memo 6A line 19

Anonymous letter from hell   Script M.Macnaghten

While entering in detail of the writing, one realizes that the finales of the "e" bent are close to the "e" of "the" of line 18 of 6B, the jamb of "y" of "only" points out that of "very" of the line 14 of 6B, the bar of "t" hooked on the right of "wate" echoes that of "the" of 15 of 6B:

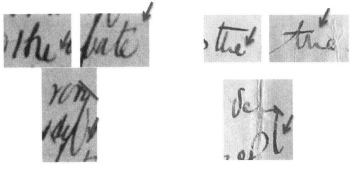

Mémo 6B

Letter From hell   / Script M.Macnaghten

Lastly, "t" with rejection of "it" and "that" have an equivalent in the regularly tilted writing of comparison, the "m" of "me" at decreasing top points out another of comparison and the "s" at concave base of "signed" is found as "Square":

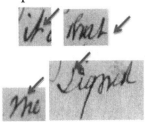

Letter From hell   / Script M.Macnaghten

All these common points are characteristics suitable for the writing of the interested party. As we can notice it, in the anonymous letter, he endeavoured to disguise the formal aspect of the writing which returns to the sources of penmanship, which is the case of anonymous writers. On the other hand, all the small personal signs which carry its brand of manufacturing have escaped him in spite of exerted control. A leopard cannot change its spots! Thus those which seek to occult their identity by disguising their writing make take.

In conclusion; Sir Melville Macnaghten is ambidextrous, and as such he writes in turn right hand and left hand. Each hand produces a perfectly homogeneous writing in its kind. It seems to hold its beautiful writing for public writing; **it is the case of the final memorandum deposited to Scotland Yard**. The written of the right hand is preserves for its personal use.

The writing full of inequalities is traced with the left hand; as on the **drafts of his memorandum; memos 6A and 6B**.

Concerning the anonymous letter coming from the hell ("From hell"); the inequalities raised in the axes of the letters and the base plate of the words let suppose, subject to the examination of the essential originals to follow with more exactitude the direction of the layout, and subject to complementary documents of comparison considering the plasticity of its graphics, which it was probably written of the left hand since these inequalities are non-existent in the neat writing of the right hand.

Suzanne Schmitt
Expert honoraire près la Cour d'Appel de Paris
et de la Cour de cassation.

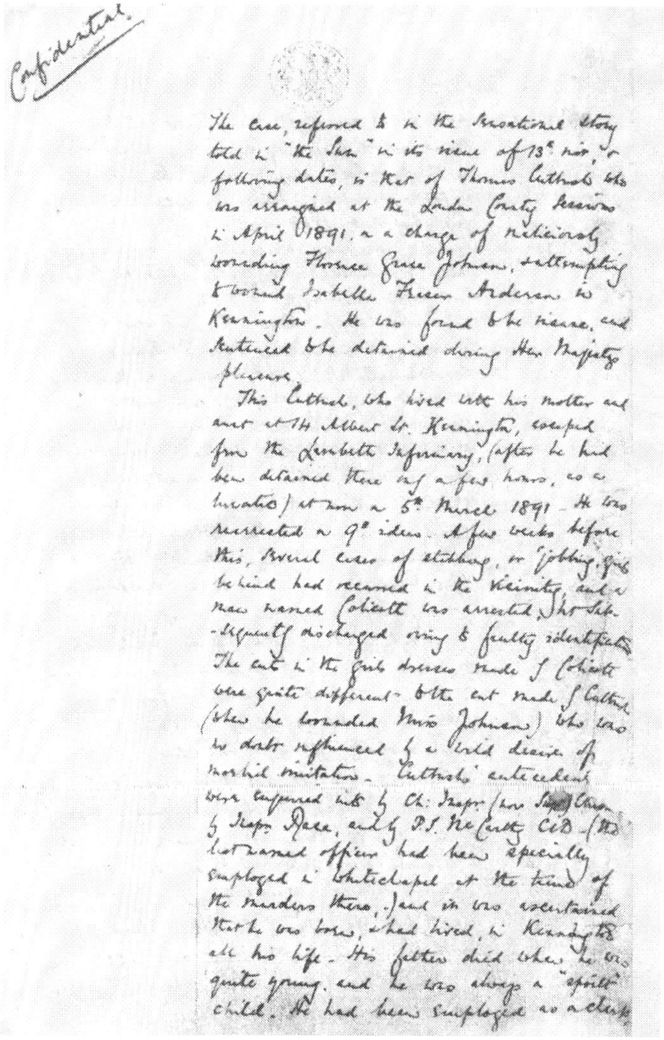

Confidential.

The case, referred to in the sensational story told in "The Sun" in its issue of 13th inst., & following dates, is that of Thomas Cutbush who was arraigned at the London County Sessions in April 1891, on a charge of maliciously wounding Florence Grace Johnson, & attempting to wound Isabella Fraser Anderson in Kennington. He was found to be insane, and sentenced to be detained during Her Majesty's pleasure.

This Cutbush, who lived with his mother and aunt at 14 Albert St. Kennington, escaped from the Lambeth Infirmary, (after he had been detained there only a few hours, as a lunatic) at noon on 5th March 1891. He was rearrested on 9th idem. A few weeks before this, several cases of stabbing, or "jabbing" girls behind had occurred in the vicinity, and a man named Colicott was arrested, but was subsequently discharged owing to faulty identification. The cuts in the girls dresses made by Colicott were quite different to the cut made by Cutbush (when he wounded Miss Johnson) who was no doubt influenced by a wild desire of morbid imitation. Cutbush's antecedents were enquired into by Ch: Inspr. (now Supt.) Chisholm by Inspr. Race, and by P.S. McCarthy CID (the last named officer had been specially employed in Whitechapel at the time of the murders there,) and it was ascertained that he was born, & had lived, in Kennington all his life. His father died when he was quite young and he was always a "spoilt" child. He had been employed as a clerk

First page of final memo filed at Scotland Yard (7pages)

reasonable suspicion. Personally, after much careful & deliberate consideration, I am inclined to exonerate the last 2, but I have always held strong opinions regarding no 1, and the more I think the matter over, the stronger do these opinions become. The truth, however, will never be known, and did indeed, at one time, lie at the bottom of the Thames, if my conjectures be correct. No 1. Mr M. J. Druitt, a doctor of about 41 years of age & of fairly good family, who disappeared at the time of the Miller's Court murder, and whose body was found floating in the Thames on 3rd Dec: i.e. 7 weeks after the said murder. The body was said to have been in the water for a month or more - on it was found a season ticket between Blackheath & London. From private information I have little doubt but that his own family suspected this man of being the Whitechapel murderer; it was alleged that he was sexually insane.

Memo 6A of M. Macnaghten

no 2 ....ski a Polish Jew, who lived in the heart of the district where the murders were committed. He had become insane owing to many years indulgence in solitary vices.. He had a great hatred of women with strong homicidal tendencies. He was (and I believe still is) detained in a lunatic asylum. about March 1889. This man in appearance strongly resembled the individual seen by the City P.C. near Mitre Square

No 3. Michael Ostrog, a mad Russian doctor &a convict & unquestionably a homicidal maniac. This man was said to have been habitually cruel to women, & for a long time was known to have carried about with him surgical knives & other instruments; his antecedents were of the very worst & his whereabouts at the time of the Whitechapel murders could never be satisfactorily accounted for. He is still alive.

And now with regard to the 3 additional murders ascribed ? by the "Sun" writer to the "Ripper".

(There follows, on p. 6.

1) The body of Martha Sh...

Memo 6B of M. Macnaghten

213

James Monro hunts the ghost of Jack the Ripper

III. The 20 questions still asked by English specialists to confirm the true identity of Jack the Ripper.

—1 Evidence indicating that the suspect was at the murder sites and could not be recognized in London:

Melville was in India until 1888 so he arrived in London in May 1888. He worked at Kearley & Tonge in Whitechapel, importing tea from his Kishnaghur property in India and lived at 9 Tite Street, Chelsea, London.

—2 A real motive for committing these crimes:

He had been impotent since May 1881 following a blow to his head. He had two children before 1881, and remained childless for seven years, and finally after the murders his wife gave birth to two more children after 1890.

Melville Magnaghten wrote this passage on pages 50 and 51 in "Days of my Years"; «One incident, however, occurred in May 1881, which changed the course of my entire life. An Indian farmer struck me on the head".

—3 Proof that he was in London at the time:

Melville Macnaghten wrote on June 5, 1888 from his home on 9 Tite Street, a letter to the Minister saying that he returned to London to take up his post at Scotland Yard and that this refusal for the job deprived him of employment for two months.

—4 Sources showing that the murderer arrived in Whitechapel before the crimes began and that he left when they stopped:

Melville arrived in London in May 1888 to carry out the 5 crimes, he stopped after Charles Warren's resignation following his fifth murder. He knew that his friend James Monro would finally manage to help him join the police.

Moreover, eating the uterus of 3 of his victims and the heart of his 5th victim cured him of his impotence. (Confirmed by new births in 1890 and 1894)

In "Days of my Years" he stated this: "he committed suicide on or about November 10, 1888, after eliminating a police commissioner".

—5 A source showing that he could have killed or killed men or animals before the killings:

He was a hunter in India and he killed and ripped a lot of jackals and wild boars in India when he was living in Kishnaghur, he would disembowel them to give the best pieces to his dogs. "Days of my Years" page 45-46 "Hunting for jackals with kangaroo dogs was the main amusement, and I killed up to seven jackals before breakfast." A jackal could be spotted not far from a field, less than three hundred yards away, we galloped in pursuit, the dogs following the horses until the forest was in sight ...»

—6 Sources showing that he did not respect the law:

He said in his letter "From Hell" that he ate the half-kidney of Eddowes and that it was very good, he confirmed his cannibalistic tendencies.

—7 Sources showing that he was a liar:

In his book "Days of my Years" he stated that he refused the police job in 1888; when in fact it was Charles Warren who finally refused it (several police documents confirm this fact).

Days of My Years page 53: *"In 1884, Mr. Monro was appointed to succeed Sir CE Howard Vincent as Deputy Commissioner of the Metropolitan Police in charge of the Criminal Investigation Department, four years later, upon my return from India, he asked me if I was willing to accept the position of Chief Constable at Scotland Yard, and if the proposal was flattering I was not able to accept it at that time because family commitments and other private matters demanded my full attention, but when the offer was made a year later, I gladly responded with the necessary formalities, and I started my job as a metropolitan police detective. "*

—8 A source indicating that he has created a false alibi:

He murdered John Druitt by smothering him like prostitutes and dragging him into the Thames with four big stones in each pocket. In 1894 in his memorandum, he used Druitt's death to make him believe he was a doctor and, that he had secret information from the Druitt family, that John Druitt was JTR.

"Days of my Years," page 53 "Although, in all likelihood, I will try to show in this chapter that Whitechapel's murderer commits suicide after the Dorset Street affair in November 1888, certain facts, highlighting this conclusion, were not in the possession of the police until a few years after I became a police officer. "

He will confirm in the 1894 memorandum that it was Druitt who was JTR.

—9 A personality that prevents him from being discovered:

James Monro covered his friend Melville Macnaghten as JTR, refusing Lawende to give the trial the description of the man he saw at Duke Street 5 minutes before the crime of Eddowes. Just as Monro dismiss James Harvey who had seen the murderer on Duke Street.

—10 A source indicating that he was known to the police:

James Monro wrote the "highly private Memorandum" by giving the name of JTR to his family.

—11 Sources giving strong hints that he confessed:

In his 1894 memorandum, he wrote: "Now the Whitechapel murderer had made five victims and only five".

A more rational theory indicates that at Miller's Court,' the murderer's brain finally gave way and then he committed suicide.

When you read "Days of my Years" it becomes obvious that the author is the person who knows the most about Jack the Ripper's crimes.

He explains that the author was a helpless maniac; that he hated women just for being women, and that the victims were the "dregs of society". Melville Macnagten says that JTR caused the fall of Charles Warren; he also said that jack the Ripper's brain gave way after the last murder of the beautiful prostitute Marie Jeanette Kelly.

—12 Personal life events explaining the crimes:

Melville Macnaghten's blow to the head in May 1881caused him to become impotent, and from that date he was unable to have children… until after the murders, in 1890.

—13 A source a few years after the killings strongly indicating that he was the killer and remembered:

"Days of my Years" by Melville Macnaghten (MM) explains everything, and gives all the details of the different murders and motives of JTR. The only lie concerns his refusal to take up his post at Scotland Yard in 1888 when he was refused by Charles Warrren. In 1987 Macnaghten's family returned the photos of the five slain prostitutes and various documents to Scotland Yard.

—14 Sources strongly explaining the choice of dates:

Before May, he had spent fifteen years in Kishnagur, India so he was unknown in London before the murders. He could walk incognito in Whitechapel, but he was sexually impotent. On the other hand, his reaction to Charles Warren's refusal and the show at the Lyceum Theater Doctor Jekkyl and Mister Hide gave a glimpse of his dual personality.

—15 Sources strongly explaining the choice of murder sites:

The first and fourth murder were carried out near his workplaces, Kearley & Co in Thomas street (near Buck's Row) and Kearley & Tonge in Mitre Square, where he had damaged the lamp post the day before the fourth murder.

—16 Sources strongly explaining killer's signature:

Melville Macnaghten strangles like a thug, and disembowels prostitutes, as he did with jackals and wild boars in India. The doctors understood that he is left-handed, but also right-handed so he is ambidextrous, MM also said in his Memorandum of 1894 "the killer was probably ambidextrous" on page 6. "The theory that Whitechapel's murderer was left-handed or, in any case, ambidextrous was rooted in the remark made by a doctor who examined the corpse of the first victims, other doctors did not agree among themselves".

—17 Sources that strongly explain his victimology:

"Days of my Years" reveals the hate Macnaghten felt for women and prostitutes. On page 56 he wrote:

"The victims, without exception, belonged to the lowest condition of female humanity, a prostitute who avoids the police and exerts all her ingenuity to stay in the darkest corners of the most deserted alleys."

"Days of my Years" pages 61 and 62:

"The man, of course, was a sex maniac, but such madness takes various forms, as we shall see later in other cases." Sexual killings are the hardest for police to bring criminals to jail for the reason that there is not only a lust for the blood, but also in many cases a hatred of the woman as a woman. Uncommonly the maniac has a sick body and what was probably the case, for Whitechapel's killer. "

—18 Sources strongly explaining the modus operandi:

By strangling his victims, he makes sure they cannot scream, and he slaughters them with a knife to finish them off. In this way, they bleed very little, which prevents him from getting covered in blood.

—19 Sources revealing his psychological problems:

Melville Macnaghten's impotence is a proven fact, because other members of his family tended to have 15 children. MM receives a blow to his head in May 1881; he can no longer have children because of sexual problems. Melville Macnaghten writes: "This blow on my head has changed all my life."

—20 "Too many coincidence" for him not to be the killer:

For the first murder, he chose Buck's Row because of its proximity to the Kearley & Co buildings (Thomas street).

Melville Macnaghten chose to commit some murders on a Saturday because of George Morris' absence from Mitre Square on that day. Indeed, every Saturday night, Morris was cleaning the accounts office in another building.

James Monro hunts the ghost of Jack the Ripper

MM / JTR after his fourth murder wait in the Kearley and Tonge building, while the police and doctors evacuate the crime scene. Then he takes a chalk on the edge of his blackboard, he also takes the half-apron of Eddowes stained with blood with which he took the uterus and the left kidney of Eddowes. And he will write more than an hour after the crime, halfway between the two crimes on Goulston Street a message linking the two crimes of this night with an anti-Semitic message, he leaves well on the half apron of Catherine Eddowes to confirm the authenticity of the message.

No doubt that MM is anti-Semitic, because he shouts Lipsky as an insult during the first murder, he confirms with his writing on the wall: "The Jews are the men who will not be blamed for nothing". The first word of the sentence written on the wall remains a mystery?

"The Juwes" A fine analysis shows that the writer has a very strong education, and that he is very clever. Indeed, the murderer was disturbed during his third murder of Stride by men who left the Socialist Club at 40 Berner Street. But MM knows from the press that on September 22, 1888, the famous poet "William Morris" had gone to Kelmscott Manor and the club to read Middle Age poems of Germanic origin. MM hopes that this sentence with this word Juwes, of medieval origin, will make it possible to make the junction with the club of the League socialist international of 40 Berner Street.

223

James Monro hunts the ghost of Jack the Ripper

IV. Index of power and Police in 1888:

Queen Victoria (1819-1901)

Minister Henry Matthews

 Private secretary Evelyn Ruggles-Brise)

Scotland Yard (4 Whitehall):

From the lowest grade to the highest:

Cadet, Constable Police (PC), Detective, Sergeant, Inspector, Chief Inspector

Superintendent, Chief Superintendent, Assistant Commissioner, Commissioner

Superintendent Charles Henry Cutbush

Chief Superintendent Thomas Arnold

Commission Sir Charles Warren Seconded by Commissioning Assistant James Monro who resigns on August 21, 1888

Sir Robert Anderson takes the post of James Monro

Chief Inspector John George Littlechild

Chief Inspector Henry Moore

Chief Inspector Donald Swanson

Inspector Frederick Aberline sent to Whitechapel Police Division H to investigate repeated murders of prostitutes.

The Whitechapel Police (H division)

Inspector Frederick Abberline seconded from Scotland Yard

Inspector Edmund Reid

Inspector Walter Beck

Inspector Joseph Henry Helson division J

Detective constable Walter Dew

Detective sergeant George Godley

Sergeant Edward Badham

PC (Police Constable) John Neil (97J)

PC James Harvey (964) met a man with Eddowes on Duke Street and should have seen the murderer in action on Mitre Square (removed on August 1, 1889)

PC Edward Watkins discovers Catherine Eddowes at Mitre Square

PC Alfred Long discovers Catherine Goulston's half-apron, as well as the writing on the wall.

V. Excerpts from Sir Melville Macnaghten's book; "Days of my Years" published in 1914:

Preface: Page 8, 9

I only owned up to two disappointments, the first being that, although I played in several trial matches, I was turned out of the Eton Eleven before the Harrow match, and the second that I became a detective officer six months after the so-called "Jack the Ripper" committed suicide, and **"never had a go at that fascinating individual."**

Chapter 1 "Births and boyhood »:

Page 1

I WAS born at Monkhams House, Woodford, on 16th June 1853, the youngest of fifteen children ('a tremendous family to provide for,' as Mr. Scrooge remarked when the ghost of Christmas stated that he had eighteen hundred brothers).

(He is referring to Charles Dickens who shows us that it is never too late to change and let the goodness that lies in each of us speak. In any case a real invitation to question and reflect on the horrors of the past.)

Page 4

The exeats were oases in the desert, and I remember full well that, arriving at home about two o'clock on the Saturday, I used to hurry over lunch, and almost invariably make my way to Madame Tussaud's and **revel in the Room of Horrors till hunger** and tea-time called me home.

The boy, seemingly, **was to be father to the man-Crime and Criminals had a weird fascination for me at a very early age**.

I used always to take away the sixpenny catalogues and study them deeply, with the result that I really remember the details of the murders committed by J. Blomfield Rush...

Chapter 4: LAYING THE GHOST OF JACK THE RIPPER»: 54 to 62

"I'm not **a butcher**; I'm not a **Yid**,

Nor yet a **foreign Skipper**,

But I'm **your own light-hearted friend**,

Yours truly, Jack the Ripper"

Although, as I shall endeavour to show in this chapter, the Whitechapel murderer, in all probability, put an end to himself soon after the Dorset Street affair in November 1888, certain facts, pointing to this conclusion, were not in possession of the police till some years after I became a detective officer.

At the time, then, of my joining the Force on 1st June 1889, police and public were still agog over the tragedies of the previous autumn, and were quite ready to believe that any fresh murders, not at once elucidated, were by the same maniac's hand. Indeed, I remember three cases

— two in 1889, and one early in 1891, which the Presubscribed to the so-called Jack the Ripper, to whom, at one time or another, some fourteen murders were attributed — some before, and some after, his veritable reign of terror in 1888.

I will deal with the terrible sobriquet of " Jack the Ripper " later on. Suffice it at present to say that the Whitechapel murderer **committed five murders, and — to give the devil his due — no more.**

... the first murder of the Whitechapel miscreant was on 31st August of that year of grace. No one who was living in London that autumn will forget the terror created by these murders. Even now I can recall the foggy evenings, and hear again the raucous cries of the newspaper boys: "Another horrible murder, murder, mutilation, Whitechapel". Such was the burden of their ghastly song; and, when the double murder of 30th September took place, the exasperation of the public at the non-discovery of the perpetrator knew no bounds, and no servant-maid deemed her life safe if she ventured out to post a letter after ten o'clock at night.

And yet this panic was quite unreasonable. The victims, without exception, belonged to the lowest dregs of female humanity, who avoid the police and exercise every ingenuity in order to remain in the darkest corners of the most deserted alleys.

I remember being down in Whitechapel one night in September 1889, in connection with what was known as the Pinchin Street murder, and being in a doss-house, entered the large common room where the inmates were allowed to do their cooking. The code of immorality in the East End is, or was, unabashed in its depths of degradation.

A woman was content to live with a man so long as he was in work, it being an understood thing that, if he lost his job, she would support him by the only means open to her.

On this occasion the unemployed man was toasting bloaters, and, when his lady returned, asked her "if she had had any luck." She replied with an adjective negative, and went on to say in effect that she had thought her lucky star was in the ascendant when she had inveigled a " bloke " down a dark alley, but that suddenly a detective, with India rubber soles to his shoes, had sprung up from behind a wagon, and the bloke had taken fright and flight.

With additional adjectives the lady expressed her determination to go out again after supper, and when her man reminded her of the dangers of the streets if he " (meaning the murderer) was out and about, the poor woman replied (with no adjectives this time), *' Well, let him come — the sooner the better for such as I/' A sordid picture, my masters, but what infinite pathos is therein portrayed!

The attention of Londoners was first called to the horrors of life (and death) in the East End by the murder of one, Emma Smith, who was found horribly outraged in Osborne Street in the early morning of 3rd April 1888. She died in the London hospital, and there is no doubt that her death was caused by some young hooligans who escaped arrest.

On 7th August the body of Martha Tabram was discovered lying on the stairs of a house in George Yard. Her death was due to a number of wounds in the chest and abdomen, and it was alleged that a bayonet had been the weapon used upon her. The evening before; she had been seen in the company of two soldiers and a female friend. Her throat was not cut, and nothing in the shape of mutilation was attempted. I think I am right in saying that the soldiers were detained, but that the available witnesses failed to identify them.

The first real "Whitechapel murder," as before stated, took place on 31st August, when Mary Ann Nichols was found in Bucks Row with her throat cut and her body slightly mutilated. This was succeeded nine days afterwards by the murder of Annie Chapman in the back yard of a house in Hanbury Street; the throat was cut in a precisely similar manner, but the mutilations were of a much more savage character. On 27th September a letter was received at well-known News Agency, addressed to the " Boss." It was written in red ink, and purported to give the details of the murders which had been committed. It was signed, "Jack the Ripper." This document was sent to Scotland Yard, and (in my opinion most unwisely) was reproduced, and copies of same affixed to various police stations, thus giving it an official imprimatur.

In this ghastly production I have always thought I could discern the stained forefinger of the journalist — indeed, a year later, I had shrewd suspicions as to the actual author. But whoever did pen the gruesome stuff, it is certain to my mind that it was not the mad miscreant who had committed the murders. The name "Jack the Ripper" however, had got abroad in the land and had "caught on"; it riveted the attention of the classes as well as the masses.

It is small exaggeration to say that little else besides these murders was talked of, leading articles appeared in nearly all of the principal papers, and feeling against the police in general, and the detective department in particular, ran very high.

When public excitement then was at white heat, two murders — unquestionably by the same hand — took place on the night of 30th September. A woman, Elizabeth Stride, was found in Berner Street, with her throat cut, but no attempt at mutilation. In this case there can be little doubt but that the murderer was disturbed at his demoniacal work by some Jews who at that hour drove up to an anarchist club in the street. But the lust for blood was unsatisfied. The madman started off in search of another victim, whom he found in Catherine Eddowes. This woman's body, very badly mutilated, was found in a dark corner of Mitre Square.

On this occasion it is probable that the police officer (James Harvey) on duty in the vicinity saw the murderer with his victim a few minutes before, but no satisfactory description was forthcoming. During this night an apron, on which bloody hands had been wiped, was found in *Gouston Street* (situated, if my memory is correct, about half-way between Berner Street and Mitre Square).

Hard by was a writing in chalk on the wall, to the effect that "The Juwes are the men *who* will not be blamed for nothing".

The apron gave no clue, and the chalk writing was obliterated by the order of a high police official, who was seemingly afraid that a riot against the Jews might be the outcome of this strange " writing on the wall.*' this was the only clue ever left behind by the murderer.

After this double murder the town had rest, forty days, and public excitement, to some extent, calmed down. But worse remained behind! On the morning of 9th November, Mary Jeanette Kelly, a comparatively young woman of some twenty-five years of age, and said to have been possessed of considerable personal attractions, was found murdered in a room in Miller's Court, Dorset Street. This was the last of the series, and it was by far the most horrible.

The mutilations were of a positively fiendish description, almost indescribable in their savagery, and the doctors who were called in to examine the remains, averred that the operator must have been at least two hours over his hellish job. A fire was burning low in the room, but neither candles nor gas were there.

The madman made a bonfire of some old newspapers, and of his victim's clothes, and, by this dim, irreligious light, a scene was enacted which nothing seen by Dante in his visit to the infernal regions could have surpassed. It will have been noticed that the fury of the murderer, as evinced in his methods of mutilation, increased on every occasion, and his appetite appears to have become sharpened by indulgence. There can be no doubt that in the room at Miller's Court the madman found ample scope for the opportunities he had all along been seeking, and the probability is that, after his awful glut on this occasion, his brain gave way altogether and he committed suicide; otherwise the murders would not have ceased. The man, of course, was a sexual maniac, but such madness takes protean forms, as will be shown later on in other cases. Sexual murders are the most difficult of all for police to bring home to the perpetrators, for "motives" there are none; only a lust for blood and in many cases a hatred of woman as woman.

235

Not infrequently the maniac possesses a diseased body, and this was probably so in the case of the Whitechapel murderer. Many residents in the East End and some in the West; came under suspicion of police, but though several persons were detained, no one was ever charged with these offences.

Only last autumn I was very much interested in a book entitled "The Lodger" which set forth in vivid colours what the Whitechapel murderer's life might have been while dwelling in London lodgings. The talented authoress portrayed him as a religious enthusiast, gone crazy over the belief that he was predestined to slaughter a certain number of unfortunate women, and that he had been confined in a criminal lunatic asylum and had escaped there from. I do not think that there was anything of religious mania about the real Simon Pure, nor do I believe that he had ever been detained in an asylum, nor lived in lodgings. I incline to the belief that the individual who held up London in terror resided with his own people; that he absented himself from home at certain times, and that he committed suicide on or about the 10th of November 1888, after he had knocked out a Commissioner of Police and very nearly settled the hash of one of Her Majesty's principal Secretaries of State.

(The word of the author on the last chapter of "Days of my Years": The final chapter that ends Melville Macnaghten's book; Days of My Years is titled TWO DINNERS TO END THE DAYS; Melville Macnaghten recounts two important meals and speaks about two men he knew well; using terms that are keys to the subject of our book.) Two evenings stand out in special prominence. One was in November 1891, on the occasion of the approaching return to India of Mr. James Monro; who had resigned the Chief Commissionership of Metropolitan Police the year before. Mr. Monro had previously been the Assistant Commissioner in charge of the Criminal Investigation Department, and I doubt whether any of the gentlemen who filled this position before or after his time ever gained more completely the affection and confidence of their officers. In him and in his judgment they believed, and knew that he would be a strong rock of defence to them in times of storm and stress.

I have no intention of ripping up healed sores, or of detailing the reasons which induced Mr. Monro to resign a post for which, by nature and by training, he was admirably fitted.

Suffice it to say that, after his retirement, he determined to revisit Bengal, to take up at his own charges some medical missionary work.

I knew that he would like to see his leading detectives once again, and I knew that the leading detectives would love to have an evening with their old and revered chief.

Mr. G. R. Sims is as amusing in private conversation as he is in public speaking, and possesses the extremely rare faculty of being brilliant on the spur of the moment, which a very different thing to firing is off carefully, prepared impromptus.

As an illustration I recall an incident which took place at the National Sporting Club some ten years ago. A boxing contest was taking place between " two likely lads '* for, I presume, the usual *' substantial purse.' The better boxer of the two was not well trained and was evidently tiring; he began to hit low, and, after being twice cautioned, was, on the occasion of a third offence, very properly disqualified. A good deal of heated discussion arose on the matter, and two of his backers came over to where Mr. Sims was standing, and said, "What do you think, Mr. Sims? We thought our man was winning hands down". "Too low down," replied G. R. S., and never smiled!

(Indeed, we can only bring this anecdote closer to the period of 1888, during which Sims wrote his articles on Jack the Ripper starting with: What we thing ... The author M. Macnaghten draws an analogy with the situation of the time and the fact that Jack the Ripper by his assassinations had caused the fall of Charles Warren.)

VI. Correspondence between Monro and Charles Warren

A thank-you to David Barrat (David Orsam) for correspondence in HO (Home Office) archives and MEPO (Metropolitan Police) archives housed in the Kew National Archives.

On April 20, 1888, from Sir Charles Warren to James Monro (HO 144/190 / A46472B):

"Minister Matthews has informed you that Mr. Macnaghten has been appointed Deputy Chief of Police, but this has caused a lot of difficulties and complications. I'll be happy if you explain to me how that happened. "

The same day, answer from James Monro

"I have been informed that the Secretary of State has approved the appointment of Mr. Macnaghten and I have communicated the fact of this approval to Mr. Macnaghten. In doing so, I followed the general practice in this matter, especially since I knew that you had approved the recommendation I had made, and that Mr. Macnaghten had asked me to keep him informed of this appointment. I am not aware of any difficulties or complications."

On May 2, 1888, from Sir Charles Warren to James Monro (MEPO 4/487):

"I think you must completely misunderstand Melville Macnaghten ... It seems that while you were working as a secret agent for the Department of the Home office, you heard from Mr. Ruggles-Brise that the secretary of the The State had approved my recommendation of Mr. Macnaghten, and, without referring or consulting me, you informed Mr. Macnaghten that the Secretary of State had appointed him deputy chief of police. So I withdrew my recommendation and I let you know. You answered that the appointment of the Secretary of State must remain to your knowledge. In fact, you have no official knowledge of the appointment of Mr. Macnaghten by the Commissioner, and as the recommendation is withdrawn, the appointment can not be made."

On May 4th, James Monro answers (MEPO 4/487):

"I regret that I can not approve these statements. To the extent that this information reaches me, I can not admit that you can give me a warning about my conduct. I am not mistaken as to the nature of the relationships I must have with you, as Commissioner, and I do not understand what gave you reason to believe otherwise.

You are mistaken when you say that while I was in the department, I heard Mr. Ruggles Brise say that the Secretary of State had approved the appointment of Mr. Macnagthen. This information was given to me by Mr. Ruggles Brise himself, in my office at 21 Whitehall Place. I communicated this decision to Mr. Macnagthen in the forms, and with the assurance that you had likewise, your recommendation to this gentleman. I was not aware of your withdrawal regarding the offer of this post to Mr. Macnaghten. I still believe that this withdrawal was later than the decision of the Secretary of State, in that your decision was communicated to me only weeks after the commission, in your memo of April 23 or 24.

Having been officially notified of the post, it seems to me that I acted in a justified manner. I do not see how I made a mistake, and by the same token, it seems impossible to do anything for me to blame myself."

On May 7, from Sir Charles Warren to James Monro (HO 144/190 / A46472B):

"I would appreciate it if in the future you were courteous enough to keep copies of your correspondence with the Home office, and if you could, as Assistant Commissioner, keep track of your verbal exchanges, keep me informed every day of what's going on."

On May 9, James Monro responds (HO 144/190 / A46472B):

"I regret not being able to follow up on your request. It seems to me that such a request is based on an error of interpretation concerning the duties inherent to my function as assistant commissioner in charge of intelligence."

On May 9, from Sir Charles Warren to Minister Henry Matthews (HO 144/190 / A46472B):

"It seems that Mr. Monro, over the last few days, has taken certain liberties without the Commissioner's consent, and ... refuses, in the future, to provide me with copies of his written or oral exchanges with the Home office. He regards my orders as a misinterpretation of his duties as Assistant Intelligence Commissioner. This declaration of independence, from Mr. Monro, is recent, and I can not see why it is based.

The Police Commissioner is responsible for the criminal investigation department as for any other police department, but I can not perform my duties if an Assistant Commissioner proclaims his autonomy. I think that this conflict of authority jeopardizes, in the meantime, the security of the Capital, and I defer to you to make it clear to Mr. Monro that as Assistant Commissioner, he must act entirely under the command of the Commissioner."

On Tuesday, June 5, 1888, Melville Macnaghten sends the following letter to the Minister:

"London 9 Tite Street"

"With regard to my appointment as assistant chief, whose request was made by Mr. Monro on March 17, and approved by Sir Charles Warren on March 19, sanctioned by yourself on March 29, 1888, I beg you want to inform me why unexplained, my assignment has not been published. I was kept on hold and unemployed for the past two months...

I believe that this appointment may be published immediately, unless satisfactory reasons for its cancellation can be attributed to me.

I have the honour to be Sir; your most obedient servant.

Signed Melville Macnaghten."

June 7 Melville Macnaghten is made aware by a letter from Minister Henri Matthews that his appointment has been denied by Charles Warren.

"Your acceptance has not been officially fulfilled and the Secretary of State, for reasons that do not concern you, has decided not to complete it, but Mr. Matthews regrets the disappointment you may have in this matter."

On June 9, Melville Macnaghten answers the following letter to the Minister:

"London 9 Tite Street"

"Sir,

In response to your letter of the current Thursday, June 7, I respect your decision, but I note that I had good reason to believe that my appointment as CID Assistant Manager was formally completed on March 29, 1888, and I was informed by a letter from Mr Monro of this appointment, date given by your private secretary to me through Mr Monro. Signed Melville Macnaghten."

June 11, Monro writes to Under-Secretary of State Minister Godfrey Lushington, Under-Secretary of State at the Home office (HO 144/190 / A46472B):

(HO 144/190 / A46472B):

"I send this official letter with regret, but the state of affairs leaves me no option. In view of the actions taken by Sir Charles Warren to peddle slanders about me, and to question my integrity, I consider myself entitled to request that I be provided with the elements that would justify such accusations, and that conduct a proper inquiry into the matter.

Regardless of the personal propensities that bind me to this case, it is my duty to point out that the problem that has been raised goes far beyond simply assigning a post from assistant to chief of police.

The accusations of Sir Charles Warren are based on the totally erroneous interpretation of my duties as assistant commissioner in charge of intelligence. In 1884 I was selected and appointed to the head of the department by the Secretary of State, and I performed these functions more successfully than my predecessor. In addition, I renounced a high office in the administration of Her Majesty the Queen for this position.

The functioning of the intelligence department, inaugurated since 1878, has never ceased to function thus, with the blessing of the various secretaries of state to succeed one another. The manoeuvres of Sir Charles Warren pervert the existing mode of operation, namely that Intelligence is under the exclusive authority of the officer in charge of it, and returns to the procedures of yesteryear, procedures condemned by the commission. The result of these manoeuvres is already visible. This change will certainly have serious consequences. As long as this problem is not solved, the intelligence department can not function properly, and these new restrictions force me to declare myself not responsible for the possible bad results that this service could produce.

I solemnly declare that the accusations of Sir Charles Warren, concerning the administration of the department, or of myself, must be the subject of a complete examination by a competent authority, knowing that it is urgent to treat the question, in view of its impact on the general interest."

"On June 20, the Secretary of State will reject the investigation." Sir Charles Warren will think that Monro is again trying to override his control, and will now call this conflict of authority a crisis.)

On July 24, from James Monro to Sir Charles Warren (MEPO 4/487):

"I was sent to town today by the Secretary of State. I wanted to go back to the office, but I was unable to do it. My health does not allow me to work, so I wish you to leave me the rest of the week, after which I propose to take my usual leave of the month of August."

On the same day Sir Charles Warren wrote to James Monro (MEPO 4/487):

"I'm sorry to hear you're sick. You can, as you propose, take leave until the end of August and I will arrange for your duties during this period to be assigned to another Deputy Commissioner."

On August 17, 1888, I wrote the following letter to the Home office: (HO 144/190 / A46472C).

"Sir, it is with great regret that I feel compelled to postpone my resignation from the office of the Assistant Commissioner, Metropolitan Police, in charge of the Criminal Investigation Department. There have been serious differences of opinion on the questions of the administration of the police between Sir Charles Warren and myself, and I feel that under a change of policy and system, which my long experience compels me to withdraw, I can not continue my mission for the efficiency of the criminal investigation department, which was specially entrusted to me by the Secretary of State in 1884 "

The resignation of James Monro was accepted by Godfrey Lushington on behalf of the Home Secretary on August 21, and he officially resigned on August 31, 1888.

James Monro hunts the ghost of Jack the Ripper

VII. Working notes:

A) The period documents consulted and used:

Dailies:

Atchison Daily Globe Kansas USA from April 23, 1888 to February 7, 1889 (21 newspapers)

Daily NewsUnited Kingdom

From 1st September 1888 to 29th December 1888 (89 newspapers)

East End News

Sept. 11, 1888; October 5, 1888, November 20, 1888 and July 19, 1889 (4 newspapers)

Parliamentary debates

November 6 to 28, 1888 and July 18 and 29, 1889 (15 debates)

Evening News London, U.K.

September 1, 1888 to December 28, 1888 (83 newspapers)

Freeman's Journal Commercial Advertiser Dublin, Ireland

September 10, 1888 to October 25, 1888 (19 newspapers)

Lloyd's weekly newspaper. (London)

April 8, 1888 and Sept. 2, Sept. 9, Sept. 22, and September 30, 1888 (5 newspapers)

Morning Advertiser (London)

September 1, 1888 to December 31, 1888 (91 newspapers)

Pall Mall Gazette

September 1, 1888 to December 12, 1888 (49 newspapers)

The Star, LONDON.

September 1, 1888 to December 24, 1888 (72 newspapers)

The Times, London

September 1, 1888 to June 3, 1901 (137 newspapers)

Sun United Kingdom

February 14, 1894 (5 newspapers)

The testimonials:

First murder Mary Ann Nichols:

Emily Holland

Testimony of the last person to have seen Mary Ann Nichols alive

Charles Cross

Testimony on the discovery of Mary Ann Nichols' body on August 31 at 3:40 am

Robert Paul

Testimony of the discovery of the body of Mary Ann Nichols August 31 at 3:45

PC 97J John Neil

Testimony of the discovery of the body of Mary Ann Nichols August 31 at 3:45

Second Annie Chapman murder:

Albert Charles Cadosh

Testimony to the crime of Annie Chapman September 8, 1888 5:18

Third murder Elizabeth Stride:

Mattew Packer

Testimony of many meetings with Jack

- Several times before the crimes, Jack buys fruit.

- September 29, 1888 purchase of a pound of black grapes with Stride at 11:20 pm

- October 27, 1888 saw Jack who threatened him and fled

Israel Schwartz

Testimony of the crime of Elizabeth Stride September 30, 1888 at 00h 45/0 h 58

Lewis Diemschultz

Testimony of the discovery of Elizabeth Stride's body September 30, 1888 at 1 hour

Fourth murder Catherine Eddowes:

Joseph Lawende, Harry Harris, Joseph Hyam Levy

Description of the meeting with Jack on September 30, 1888 at 1:30

George Morris

Testimony of Kearley and Tonge Warden September 29 and 30, 1888

The writing and the half-apron on Goulsont Street:

PC 254 Alfred Long and Constable Detective Daniel Halse

Discovery of the half-apron and writing on the wall of September 30, 1888 at 2 h 55

Edmund Reid Head of H whitechapel division

Copy the writing: The Juwes are the men that will not blamed for nothing

Fifth murder Mary Jane Kelly:

Testimony of George Hutchinson, who is the last person to have spoken to Mary Jane Kelly, and attended the meeting with Jack, followed the couple Jack and Mary Jane Kelly until she entered Miller's court. It gives a very precise description of Jack

Testimony of the person Elizabeth Prater who heard Mary Jane Kelly cry at 4 hour (the time of the murder).

Testimony of owner John McCarthy of Mary Jane Kelly's room

Testimony of employee Thomas Bowyer who discovered the body.

B) Sir Melville Macnaghten 'Days of my Years'

Memoirs written in 1914 and published in London and New York.

a) He writes at the end of chapter 4: the murderer's motive was to force the resignation of the unpopular "Charles Warren".

b) But in this story we understand that his second mobile is: "Finding a libido lost in May 1881 in India" because of a blow to the head, which stopped his offspring to two children, Charles Melville born November 18, 1879 and Julia Mary last child conceived before the blow on the head in February 1881 and which will be born on September 10, 1881.

A period of 7 years will pass without children; Melville is powerless and unfortunate; when he arrived in London he learns that Charles Warren refuses entry into the police.

C) Memorandum written by Melville Macnaghten of February 14, 1894

This memorandum exists in two manuscript versions written by Melville. Melville says the murderer is ambidextrous. The letter 'From Hell' is written with the left hand. Suzanne Schmitt expert in writing confirms the ambidextrous.

Melville gives three suspects, including Montague John Druitt who would be the No. 1 suspect

He ends with this sibylline sentence:

"The truth, however, will never be known, and did indeed at one time lie down the Thames, if my conjunctions be correct"

The truth, however, will never be known, and will indeed, if my feeling is right, be a lie at the bottom of the Thames. (Druitt at the bottom of the Thames)

D) The English National Archives of Kew:

Special thanks to Mr. David Barrat (David Orsam) for his help with the HO archives (Home Office) and the MEPO (Metropolitan Police) archives that are housed in the Kew National Archives.

(HO 144/190 / A46472B) (MEPO 4/487) (MEPO 2/22) (MEPO 3/182)

E) Literature:

Strange Case of Dr. Jekyll and Mr. Hyde

Robert Louis Stevenson New York 1886 the play will be played several days from August 4, 1888 at 'London Lyceum theatre'

A WISER WOMAN? A BOOK OF MEMORIES

Christabel Aberconway edited Hutchinson & Co. UK 1966

Written by the daughter of Melville Macnaghten

FROM HELL

Alan Moore et Eddie Campbell une autopsie de Jack l'Éventreur

Traduit en français par J.P. Jennequin Édition Delcourt 2000

Jack The Ripper (The Theories and the facts)

Colin Kendell Amberley Publishing 1988-2012

The complete Jack the Ripper A to Z

Paul Begg Martin Fido Keith Skinner 2010

The John George Littlechild Letter to G.R. Sims September 1913

Weather Conditions for the Nights of the Whitechapel Murders. Courtesy of Casebook Productions

Saturday night in the east end

F) Anonymous letters:

a) The letter from "From Hell" (the only one written by the murderer with his left hand)

Addressed to George Lusk accompanied by the half-kidney of Catherine Eddowes to confirm its authenticity.

b) Collection of 50 anonymous letters (out of 350 to 600, received by the police)

The first "Dear Boss" of September 25, 1888 was written by two journalists (Thomas Bulling and Frederick Best).

Like the second "Saucy Jack" of October 1, 1888

All other anonymous letters are addressed mainly to Charles Warren under the name "Dear Boss" and signed "Jack the Ripper".

These letters were written by a multitude of Londoners, some of whom were discovered by the police and others by investigators, for example Walter Sickert by Patricia Cornwell.

G) The Casebook website and its forum of "Ripperologist":
Suspects:
Discussion of the different people who have been suggested as Jack the Ripper Victims.

H) Patricia Cornwell in her book and research on the murder weapon:

"Jack the Ripper Case Ranked" Patricia Cornwell (Edition of Two Lands 2002). After researching and testing the different pieces of meat on a piece of meat. Ms. Cornwell concluded that the most effective weapon was Kukri (p.534); Blade of 16 to 20 cm forming a bend forward. A man returning from Calcutta could have brought back this type of knife.

I) Sophie Herfort in 2007 gives for the first time the name of the culprit:

First edition (Tallandier 2007) 'Jack the Ripper unmasked, the definitive investigation'. Sir Melville Macnaghten would be the serial killer, the motive being to provoke the resignation of Sir Charles Warren so that James Monro could take his place and bring Melville Macnaghten into the police.

In 2008 at 'Dockland's Museum of London', a plaque indicates that Sir Melville MacNaghten 1853-1921, visited all crime scenes, and kept in his office the photos of the victims of 'Jack the Ripper'. Photos and documents that the family of his daughter Marie Christabel sent back to Scotland Yard in 1987.

'Dockland's Museum of London'

Plaque at the Dockland's museum in London indicating that Sir Melville Macnaghten had abnormal professional behavior.

Thanks

In 1968 a radio reported that the identity of the first serial killer "Jack the Ripper" was still an enigma. I heard my father say, **Jack the Ripper must be a Policeman!**

In 2011 a TV show, said that a policeman from Scotland Yard was Jack the Ripper. Intrigued, I bought on Abe Books; his biography appeared in 1914 "Days of my Year". The adventure begins by reading this book and finding on the Internet, newspapers and documents of time including the famous letter 'From Hell'. I compile all the documents and I can trace exactly the life of this policeman and the crossings with the different murders. The book takes shape, and a meeting with Cedric Neuser and Vincent Palacio, allows forming a credible story, romanticized by Vincent. To both of you, a big thanks.

A few years later, my wife Sophie made first corrections, supplemented by Josiane Gaggero, Séverine Roure, and Isabelle Teboul.

What patience, their support has been precious to me!

The cover is entrusted to Christian Roure who did an admirable job staging: the murder weapon, the Tower of London and ... Sir Melville. Bravo the artist!

A first edition is drawn on Amazon, but the first readers packed by history confirm that this book is not sufficiently mature: thank you for their advice.

It is the meeting with Nicole Deroin, who gives a final touch to the construction of the book and the final corrections necessary. This book could not have existed without the expertise of Suzanne Schmitt, who gives unstoppable proof.

My son Sébastien and my daughter Nathalie support me with their joie de vivre and exciting sports activities.

To all my family and friends, once again, a big affectionate thank you.

Table

Attachments:

James Monro hunts the ghost of Jack the Ripper

James Monro hunts the ghost of Jack the Ripper

Printed in Great Britain
by Amazon

38136808R00148